GREYLAND

D.U.M.B.s
(Deep Underground Military Bases)

Book 1

David Sloma

Copyright © 2013 David Sloma
All rights reserved.

This is a work of fiction. Any resemblance to any person, place, product, government, or thing is purely coincidental.

www.DavidSloma.com

Published by Web of Life Solutions
www.weboflifesolutions.com

Cover design by Melchelle Designs
www.melchelledesigns.com

Available as a paperback and an ebook

ISBN: 149286756X
ISBN-13: 978-1492867562
April 19, 2018 version

THANK YOU

For reading

1

Leon Verdat loved dirt. As a child he used to be fascinated with sandboxes and would spend lots of time in them, building roads for his toy cars and dump trucks. The happy, thin, black-haired American boy would destroy the sand roads he had made, and bury the cars, only to mount brave rescue missions with his plastic soldiers and the tiny medical team (that came with their own stretcher which fit into the toy ambulance). When the siren on top of the ambulance was pressed, it rang out with an alarm, which lent urgency to his rescue missions. Many were the times that his parents had to coax him in from playing for dinner, and then get all of the dirt off him before he could eat.

His father was an accountant, and his mother was a stay-at-home mom, in a time when that was widely possible on a single salary. His parents came from a hard-working, European background (Irish and German), and instilled solid morals and a strong work ethic in him. He grew up in the 1950s, in Kansas, and spent a lot of time thinking about science and the quickly changing world around him – and he always wondered at the bad side of science that had him ducking under his desk at school for nuclear bomb drills.

His friends liked to go with him on hikes around the surrounding hills, as he had the uncanny knack of always finding nice gemstones. Sometimes, they found large storm drains, and they could wiggle past the metal barricades and go exploring inside the tunnels. Finding the tunnels was like finding another world for Leon, and he became an avid spelunker soon after.

When they got back from their hikes, he and his friends always had pockets full of amethyst and other rocks he had found for them. They'd hide the stones in the big sandbox, burying them in many spots, and he would manage to find them, with amazing success, sometimes even with his eyes closed! No one knew how he did it.

Later, when he was in his teens, Leon moved to building sand castles on the beach, and entering in competitions. Those were good for impressing the girls, he found, as when he won, he got his picture in the local newspaper and got a trophy. Truth be told though, he had almost as much fun knocking the castles down afterward, and returning the sand to its natural state, where anything was possible, again. But as long as he could get his hands into the sand, and dirt, and feel its texture and smell its smell, that was fine with him.

When he was in high school, he worked for a landscaper and thought he might start a business in that field. But when he was looking at courses to take at college, he found out about people who built tunnels deep underground for a living, and his love for the dirt increased into a passion for a career he could do for the rest of his life. He studied pedology, and engineering, so he could become an expert in soil and building underground. He then became an apprentice with a construction company that specialized in tunnel building, so he learned all he could about underground construction techniques there.

Within a few years of graduation he was running his own successful construction business in a rural part of New York State, specializing in underground construction, mainly of tunnels. His work underground led him to develop a fascination with geodes, and he found many of them on his work sites. He became a collector and expert in them, attending trade shows, and even giving talks on the stones to groups of local enthusiasts. It was at one of these gem shows that he met his future wife. For him, being able to be underground, and work with the soil and stones was a dream come true. He lived his dream for many happy years, until one day an unexpected visitor to his office changed all that.

"You want me to build underground bases? For the shadow government? With the secret military?" Leon asked the Man in Black who sat across from him.

The man was thin with beady black eyes, pale skin, and slicked down black hair, like men used to wear when Leon was a child. His suit was old fashioned too, with a thin black tie. His shoes were also of a decades old style, but new-looking and highly polished.

"Not so loud Mr. Verdat, the walls tend to have ears," the man said, smiling faintly.

As the man spoke, Leon felt suddenly sleepy. The man's voice was mildly hypnotic, and Leon suspected he was using some sort of mentalist's programming technique on him.

"How do I know this is legit? You won't even give me your name, just Mr. Black!" Leon blinked his assertive green eyes, which were bugging out.

"It's better that way. How could you prove who I was anyway, no matter what name I gave you?" the man cooed. "Besides, this is just a preliminary visit to...gauge your interest in our proposal."

"I see." Leon shook himself back fully awake and drank some coffee.

This guy's an asshat, Leon thought.

The man had said that he represented a secretive, military branch of the shadow government, the true government, not the one Leon and most people knew about.

Mr. Black shifted in his seat and pulled out a cigarette case. It was old, and ornate looking, like something from the 1940's, stylish with a flourish of Art Deco. He opened it to reveal a neat line of cigarettes. "Do you mind if I smoke?"

"No, go ahead," said Leon, opening the window behind his desk. He settled back in his chair as Mr. Black lit the cigarette and puffed out a billow of smoke that rose above their heads. They both watched the smoke rise. It quickly disappeared with the breeze coming in from the window. It was a warm spring day and the air carried the aroma of cut grass and flowers. "I've been building tunnels and underground structures for a long time. Don't you think I've have come across some of these "secret, underground military bases" by now, in my line of work?"

"No. Not unless you had been cleared to see them."

"Like how?"

"Security cleared. This is not a child's game, Mr. Verdat; this is serious business."

"Well, I've heard there were underground cities, too, but I've never seen proof of any of them. I *have* seen some very large bomb shelters in my work; even built many. If you want me to build you a shelter, there's no need to go through this cloak and dagger routine..."

"No, we want you to work on one of our underground bases."

"Bases. Right."

"If you are interested to assist us, then you will receive a visit from a high-ranking officer in the secret military. The fine details of your contract will be reviewed, and there will be papers to sign. You will be required to pass a security clearance and swear an oath of secrecy; both things you will have no trouble doing, as you are a good, hard-working, law abiding family man."

His face went taught and he narrowed his eyes. "You mean, you've been spying on me, already."

The man took a delicious puff on his cigarette, let it out, and smiled. "Why, of course. Why do you think I'm here? We know a great deal about you. We think you are our kind of people, and that you would be of great service to us. And, to your country. You want to help your country, don't you?"

He swallowed, hard. If the man really represented the powerful group he claimed he did, then he knew there was only one correct answer to the question. "Of course I do. But why me?" The man was not really asking him, but telling him, just in a gentle way, he knew.

Mr. Black gestured with his cigarette, and looked around the wood-paneled office, the walls of which were covered with framed covers from engineering magazines, letters of commendation from city officials, and thanks from many charities. "You are one of the best in your field. One of the brightest engineers, with extensive tunnel-building experience – one of the most sought after. Your business has done very well. You have clients from all over the world, and you are in constant demand. You worked on the Chunnel. That's quite a feat."

Leon nodded. "It was. There were some days I didn't think we'd be able to get it finished, but we did. It's an amazing accomplishment."

"Precisely! That's why we want you to come and work for your country, Mr. Verdat."

"In secret."

"That's right. Doing the sort of work you do, I don't think it's a complete surprise to you that these groups exist, and that they've been building secret, underground facilities for a long time."

"But I've never worked for the military before. I don't know if that's something I'm interested in doing. I'm a peaceful person. And, please call me Leon."

"Alright, Leon." The man sucked deep on his cigarette, burning it almost down to the filter, then he then let it drop to the floor, as there was no ashtray. He ground out the butt with his shiny shoe. "Enough of this chit-chat. Let me tell you how this is going to work, *Leon*. You will come to work for us. You will do a good job, you will be highly paid – more money than you've ever made – and you will keep quiet about your work. That includes not saying anything to anyone about our visit, here and now. Do I make myself clear?"

"Yes, but I don't know if I want to..."

"Mister Verdat...Leon," the man smiled. "You've got such a nice, thriving business going here. It would be a shame if it were to run into troubles and go bankrupt. What would you do then to provide for your lovely family? Jennie is going to have her fifth birthday party next week."

Leon sat back and considered the man's words carefully. He took a few breaths. He was trapped and he knew it. He had to find a way to cooperate. "I'm sure we can work something out."

"Excellent, Leon. Excellent!" Mr. Black stood up and extended his hand.

Leon shook it, weakly, and forced a smile, feeling sick in his stomach.

"Welcome aboard! Have a good evening. We'll be in touch," the man turned and left the room.

Leon got up and followed him out of his deserted office, and locked the front door. He watched the man get into an old, but perfectly preserved black Lincoln and start up its large engine. The car rumbled to life and its headlights flashed on. He watched as the car slipped away down the street, the red taillights fading away into darkness.

"Well, then," he said to himself. He sat down at his desk and put his hands behind his head. He looked at the framed articles and plaques on the walls, his eyes coming to rest on a family picture of him, his wife Mary, and their daughter Jennie.

Finally, he sighed and got up to go home, knowing his life was about to change in ways he couldn't control. He had heard rumours of secret, underground building projects, but they had been just stories, until today.

Turning out the lights, he walked to the front door and set the alarm. Once outside, he turned the key, then tried the handle to make sure it was locked. He looked around the parking lot and street, but there was no one in sight.

He got into his black Mercedes SUV and started it up. He pulled out into the quiet street, and checked his mirrors to see if he was being followed. He saw no one, but that didn't mean they hadn't put a tracking device on his car and were monitoring his movements on a computer screen from a remote location.

He drove for a while, around the downtown, not wanting to go home just yet. He needed some time to cool his jets and to think. He looked at the people walking around as he drove past; they looked free. But he didn't feel free any longer.

***

Leon pulled into the circular driveway of his luxury home and parked beside his wife's SUV, which was also a Mercedes, the same top-of-the-line model as his, except in white; a matching pair. He put on a big smile before walking to the door to his wife and daughter. Mr. Black had kept him at work late, but then again, Leon had been working a lot of overtime lately.

"How'd work go, hon?" Mary asked him as he stepped in the house. She gave him a kiss, his loving wife, always happy to see him, despite his small faults.

"Fine, just fine," he said and hugged her.

Not really fine, no, but you can't know that. At least, not yet. Maybe one day.

"Sorry I missed dinner. I had a client come by just as I was about to leave and we had some issues to discuss."

"Oh, nothing too serious, I hope?" She looked him over, attuned to the tension on his face and body. She put a hand on his back and gave him a gentle massage.

"Naw, I can handle it," he smiled, rubbing the back of his neck, until Mary took over.

I hate not being able to tell her what's going on!

Their daughter Jennie came running up to him and grabbed his legs in an embrace. "Daddy, daddy!" she yelled.

"Hi, there!" He picked her up and hugged her. "Daddy missed you very much today."

He visited with her for a while, getting caught up on the events of her young life. But not for long, as it was late, and near her bedtime. So, he carried her to her bedroom, tucked her into bed with a story, and she was asleep before long.

He then ate his warmed up dinner as he spent some time flipping through the TV channels. There was not much on to interest him, not even a new Breaking Bad episode. Mary sat with him and ate some desert, chocolate crumble, one of his favourites, that she had made. She told him about her day, and he tried to pay attention, but his day had been pretty eventful itself, and he found it hard to listen to her, the thoughts in his head, and the TV at the same time.

***

Leon lay in bed after trying to make love to his wife, unable to sleep. He blamed his inability to perform on stress and lack of sleep, and that was mostly true. He *was* very stressed out from the visit with Mr. Black earlier that day, and he often had sleep problems, anyway. But sexual dysfunction was a rare thing for him. He was healthy for a man in his mid-forties, with a strong libido, and his wife, a few years younger, was quite attractive. It was just not the best thing for his mind to be visited by an agent of the secret government and be asked, rather forced, to work for them, he felt.

Goddam world caving in on me...

Mary was understanding about his "problem" that night, and as it rarely happened, she didn't question him further. He knew that if it were to continue she would have questions, and he dearly hoped that didn't happen. He had not mentioned anything to her about Mr. Black's visit, and he doubted he ever would, or could. He knew that if he did end up working for the secret government, building their underground bases, he'd never be able to tell his family.

Goddammit!

He twisted on the bed and gripped his pillow tight. His eyes searched the darkness of the bedroom and settled on the tree branches of autumn that shook in the wind outside the window.

He went down to the kitchen to get a midnight snack. He knew it was a bad idea to eat at night, with him being overweight, but maybe it would calm his nerves, and churning stomach.

He took the milk out of the fridge and poured a tall glass. It felt good going down and did help settle his stomach some. As he drank, he looked out the kitchen window and thought he saw a figure moving in the back of his yard. He almost spit out the milk, which he knew he really shouldn't be drinking, anyway, if he was concerned about losing weight. He put the glass down on the counter as quietly as he could.

Stepping lightly to the sliding door, he peered outside. He didn't see anyone. But he supposed, if there were secret government-type agents spying on him, they'd likely be pretty skilled and hard to spot. He leaned back on the doorframe, his heart pounding in his ears.

"I don't need this shit," he whispered. Thoughts came into his mind of just packing up and moving to another country, as far away as he could get.

He sat at the kitchen table for a long time, in the dark, looking out the sliding doors. He never saw anyone.

As the dawn started to break he felt very tired, and climbed back upstairs to Mary in bed. At least he might be able to get a couple of hours of sleep, if he was lucky.

2

Leon entered his office building and tried to act like nothing was wrong. Nancy, the receptionist was already at her desk. She came in early, usually before everyone and opened the place up. He grabbed one of the donuts that she had brought in, a Friday tradition.

"Morning, Nancy," he said, taking a bite of a cruller and pouring himself a coffee.

"Good morning. There's a man waiting for you in your office."

He felt a wave of dread go through him. His mind raced and his stomach knotted up. "Oh, yeah? Who is it?"

"He just said he was a friend and that you'd know what it was about."

Leon nodded, trying to keep his composure, "Ah, yes. Thanks. Hold my calls for now."

"Yes, boss." She went back to typing on the computer.

He stirred the cream and sugar into his coffee slowly, then shuffled to his office. He could see a man's crew cut head though the window of the door as he approached. As he entered, he saw a well-built man in his fifties, he guessed, wearing an expensive tan suit.

The man stood as Leon entered. "Hello, I'm General Simpson. Nice to meet you, Leon," the man extended a beefy hand.

"Thank you, likewise." He shook the man's hand, then closed the door and settled in behind his desk.

The General sat back down in the chair in front of the desk and smiled.

"I was wondering how long it would take you to show up," Leon said, trying to sound jovial.

"How's that?"

"Nothing, just making a joke. I suppose you're here because of...Mr. Black?"

Like that's his real name.

"That's right. I know he briefed you on our proposal. I'm here to make the formal presentation, and if you agree, then I have some papers for you to sign. Ask any questions you want. If I can't answer them, due to security reasons, I'll let you know."

He had a hundred questions running through his mind, but picking one was difficult. Immediately, his thoughts went to his business, his earnings, and his family. "What happens to my business if I'm working on projects with you? Do I have to go away for a long time on-site? What about my income?"

"Not to worry. You'll be given a generous salary, plus bonuses, and make more than you're making now. You will be working here and there, but you'll be able to come home on a regular basis, and even keep running your business. But if we need you, we expect you to make us your first priority."

"I see," murmured Leon. He drank some coffee and let it all sink in. "You'll pay me more than I make with my business? You are going to guarantee that?"

"Yes, we will. In writing. You will receive a signing advance, and a regular paycheque. If the projects you head up finish ahead of schedule and under budget, you'll receive a bonus."

He smiled. "A signing advance? I feel like a football player getting recruited, or something."

"It's not that far off, Mr. Verdat. You have skills and talents that we require. If we don't recruit you and pay you well, someone else might. We'd lose the benefit of your skills. We wouldn't want that; we hate to lose, and usually never do." The General looked him straight in the eye.

"I'd have to keep it all secret, right? No telling anyone."

"Top secret. Actually, above that. And, that's right, you will be bound by a security oath. If you disclose any details of the jobs you work on, you could face imprisonment for twenty years, or more. It's not a good idea to talk about any work you do with us, to anyone."

"It sounds very serious. And, I'd take it as serious. I'm just not sure it's something I want to get into. I have a successful business here. Things are going well. I'm happy, and my family is happy. Why would I want to change and jeopardize all that? All that I have built in my life so far? Tell me that, General. I mean, I support my country and all, and I'm all for freedom, but I'm not a military person. No offense."

The General leaned back and looked him over. "None taken. We knew going into this that you were not going to be easily persuaded. Some agents in our own forces, but mostly abroad, resort to...unpleasant means to recruit talent. I don't want to go down that path with you, despite what Mr. Black may have indicated. So, rest assured, we are not here to blackmail you. What good would you be to us then, working under duress? No, that is not our way. What you need to understand is that coming on board with us is necessary for our country's survival, and perhaps the survival of the entire world. But I cannot disclose further details to you until you have signed the security oath, and received your security clearance. The situation is dire. We need your help."

Leon downed his coffee. "What could be so bad? I'd have heard about it on the news? What's the problem? You guys have great engineers working for you already."

The General laughed a little. "Don't believe all that's on the news. And, what about the things that don't make the news? I know of many important, secret operations that the vast majority of the public has never heard about. We do have some great people working with us, but we need a lot more. There is a big push on to construct more underground facilities. You've heard of global warming, I'm sure."

"Of course."

"Well, events related to that could happen that render our government, both public and secret, unable to function. We need more subterranean bases built and we need them fast. I'm in possession of recent intelligence information that says some major calamities are in store for our planet and we need to take all the precautions we can to maintain our global position of strength, military supremacy, if you will, and continuance of government should any of these events take place. And, they will take place, Mr. Verdat. For the good of you, your family, your country, and your planet, it would be in all of those best interests to sign on with what I am offering you. You'll learn more later, and let me tell you, what you will learn will shock and frighten you, but it's the truth." He lifted his briefcase onto his lap and tapped it. "Shall we look over the paperwork?"

Leon nodded, and the man turned the locks on the case and took out a thick folder. He handed it over.

"Take your time. Read it carefully. Where can I get some coffee in this joint?" The General stood up and smoothed out his clothes.

"Uh, just down the hall. My receptionist will get you anything you need."

"Thanks," said the General, and he went off in search of coffee.

Leon flipped through the many pages and felt a headache coming on.

***

After he had read through all the pages, Leon picked up a pen and signed.

What choice do I have? I say no, who knows what could happen? Though, if there's a way I can help the world out of some problems...

He pushed the papers toward the General, who signed as well.

Then, the General had Leon recite an oath that he would not divulge any details of his employment, under severe penalties, so help him God.

The oath finished, the General smiled, and he looked genuinely proud. "I hereby declare you are now sworn in and you have been granted a provisional Top Secret clearance, as we have already done your background check. Your level will eventually increase to 15 above Top Secret, in time, but that's good enough for now."

"There's levels above Top Secret?"

The General chuckled. "Oh, yes. Many more. Even the President of our country is not cleared for them all!"

"Wow!"

"Many Presidents have tried to gain access to our secret bases and uncover the truth about UFOs, and they never got it; their security clearance was just not high enough."

"Oh, my God!"

"You should consider yourself privileged. It's a fascinating world you are now entering!"

"I'll say."

"Your view of things will never be the same again, after some time with us."

"I'm ready!"

"Good! Then, welcome to the Diggers 18th! That's the name of your team. The formalities are to come, such as issuing you an ID, but consider yourself in your country's service." He offered his hand and they shook.

"Thank you," Leon said. He actually did feel a small bit of national pride, and also wonder. "So, just how high do the security clearances go?"

"Up over 37 levels, and then there are even special levels above that. You've got a lot to learn, young grasshopper," the General winked. He then handed Leon a package marked "Top Secret."

For a moment, Leon just stared at it, unmoving.

"Go ahead. Open it. You need to become familiar with what you'll be dealing with down there."

Leon opened the package and took out an envelope with reports, photos, mechanical drawings, engineering plans, soil reports, and blueprints. The papers gave an overview about the construction and current state of a secret underground base, its location not stated, and plans for its expansion. He started to scan the documents, but stopped cold when he saw the words "alien race" and "extraterrestrial contact."

"Aliens? Like little green men? Are you kidding me here?" He put down the papers and tried to laugh it off, even though his twisting gut told him there was more to the story.

"It's no joke," the General said, stone-faced. "We've been visited by an alien race. And, we're at war."

"You mean like all those people who say they've been abducted?"

"That's part of it, yes."

"So, that's real? All those stories about people being taken by aliens, out of their bedrooms, and into their ships and anally probed? Come on!"

The General shifted in his seat and folded his hands in his lap, "Do you think all of the millions of reports of UFO sightings and abductions are just pure lies? BS made up by delusional people? And, all the photographic evidence, that's all fake?"

"Probably...some grainy photos, I mean..."

"Really? And, of all the billions of planets out there, billions upon uncountable billions, that ours is the only one with intelligent life? I'm here to tell you that aliens are real, and we've had contact with them."

"This I need to see!"

"Yes, you do. And you will, but for now I'll give you the short version." The General proceeded to talk and Leon listened, having a hard time believing what he was being told.

***

Hours later, Leon shook hands with the General in the lobby of his office. The briefing had taken all day, and the office was empty. It was dark outside.

"I hope that was not too much information for you to process at once, Leon. But it's my job to bring you up to speed on what's really going in. You need to know to do your job effectively. Believe me, there's plenty you have not been told; there are vast secrets that are on a need to know basis, only. Some of them you may learn in time, many you will not. Just as there are things I know, and things I won't get to know. It's the nature of the job. Have a good night, and we'll be in touch soon," the General turned and left.

Leon watched him go and get into a limousine that had just pulled up. Then, he locked up the front door and poured another cup of coffee. It was old coffee, but it was still warm, and a lot of sugar and cream made it palatable. He went back into his office to look over the documents the General had given him. He was dying to call up Mary and his friends, and tell them that aliens and UFOs were real, but thoughts of a military prison, and financial ruin soon dampened his enthusiasm.

He looked at the phone, knowing he should call his wife and at least let her know he was on his way home. He'd have to break the news to her about the new contract, that he'd have to go away for a while, but that was all he was allowed to tell her; no specifics. It was going to be tough keeping all the juicy bits to himself, but it was a necessity.

I've got a country, and a planet to help save!

He grinned as he dialed her. "This *is* kinda fun," he admitted to himself. "The pay is nice too!"

He left his office whistling, with the Top Secret folders under his arm. Just as he was about to get into his SUV, he stopped. He looked around and gripped the folders, his heart beating in his eardrums, feeling his blood pressure rise. But no one was in sight. He turned around, went back into the office, and opened up his personal safe.

"That was close, Leon," he said as he spun the dial around. "Be more careful!" He locked the folders inside the safe, instantly feeling better that they were in there. If he had let those papers get into the wrong hands, it would not go well for him. It wouldn't do to have an inquisitive wife asking questions about

Top Secret documents, or a playful young daughter go tearing through them.

He walked carefully out of his office, made sure all the lights were off, that the alarm system was on, and that the front door was locked. He tired the handle just to be sure, as he always did. But this time he gave it an extra yank. He stopped and peered through the glass to confirm that the glowing LEDs of the alarm system were on like they should be.

He put the key into the ignition and started his car, the last one in the lot. He looked around, feeling nervous, but not sure of what.

Being followed? Watched?

He drove home more slowly than usual. The secrets the General had told him were nagging away in his mind, and he didn't think he'd be able to bear them alone. He was going to have to tell Mary everything, but it would have to be at the right time. It wouldn't be long before the big cheques started arriving, and he was called away to field locations for days, or weeks at a time. He just hoped she'd understand why he couldn't have asked her first; it was not as if he'd really had a choice to say no.

She'd probably argue that he did have the right to say no, that it was a free country after all, and things like that, he knew. But he also knew better than to try and talk her out of her views. Maybe she'd come around in time to seeing the truth of the situation, he hoped.

He got home late for dinner, but it was still warm in the oven - lasagna. Mary was used to him often working late, and most of the time he didn't even call to let her know, it was just a given. She'd taken to preparing food that could easily be kept warm, or reheated. She wasn't overjoyed that he spent too much time at work, but they had a good lifestyle, so she supposed the sacrifices were worth it.

"Hi, babe," he kissed Mary hello.

"Hiya. How'd it go today?"

That simple question, asked thousands of times had never filled him with so much dread before. "Just fine. Jennie's in bed?"

"Yeah, she was tired so I let her go to bed early."

He nodded and sat down at the table, then shoveled pasta into his mouth. "Good, good. How are you doing?"

She shrugged. She was feeling lonely, and a bit neglected lately, but didn't think it would do much good to mention it to him. They'd had several conversations about the lack of time he spent with her, but it never did any good. Maybe one day she'd leave him, when Jennie was a bit older. She wasn't sure yet. It was not something she wanted to do, but a lot of the time it seemed he was married to his job and not her. "Fine. I was busy running around doing errands, taking care of the house and Jennie. Then, I made dinner. That sort of thing."

He stopped eating and took a drink of wine. "Honey, there's something I've got to tell you. It's work-related, and I don't think you're going to like it. But hear me out. It's going to bring in a lot more money for us, though. I know that's something we'll all enjoy." He was sure that would be a good set-up for the news he had to deliver.

She put down her fork and dabbed her mouth with the linen napkin that she had picked out at the fancy housewares store, during one of her many solo shopping trips. "What is it?" She took the glass of wine in her hand and sipped at it, suddenly nervous and frightened.

"Well..." He took a deep breath, "I've been given a new contract by the government, for a military project, and..."

"Military? What are you doing with them?"

"They came to me. It's not like I could have easily refused."

"Sure you could have."

"Well, that's up for debate. But I'll be starting it soon and I'll have to go away for it."

"I knew it."

"Not for long, though, I don't think. Anyway, there will be a lot more money coming in as a result, as much, or even more than I'm making now, while only doing this part-time. The rest of the time I'll continue with my own business, as usual." He sat back and watched her reaction.

She didn't say anything at first, just drank more wine, emptying her glass. "More money, is great, that's true. But it sounds like

Jennie and I are going to see you even less than we do now. I don't know why you said yes. We've talked about this sort of thing, about you having to go away. I thought you were going to stop doing that, and work less hours? Jennie is growing up so fast, you know? And, you're missing a lot of that. Now, you're going to be missing even more."

He shook his head and put his glass down with a solid clunk. "Weren't you listening? It's not like I really had a choice! Sure, they said I had a choice, but did I really? What would have happened to my business had I said no? It wasn't an offer, honey, despite what you might think. They wanted me to work for them, and that was that. I don't see how I could have turned them down."

She gathered up the plates and took them into the kitchen, her long, brown hair floating by him. "I don't understand, Leon. I really don't. What means more to you, us, or work?"

"I-I..." he stammered, lost for words and watched her walk away. "Don't be like this, come on, honey."

The plates were dropped into the sink much more roughly than usual.

That night in bed, Mary slept on her side, facing away from him.

3

Life returned to relative normal for Leon and his family for the next few weeks, as fall settled in and Jennie went back to school. He had spent as much time with his family as he could that late summer, before being called away on his mystery job. He and Mary took Jennie out a lot more often to parks, ice cream shops, and just to drive around together looking at the leaves changing colours.

He made an effort to leave work early and get home for dinner almost every night. Mary and his daughter both seemed much happier that he was spending more time with them. He liked it too, and just wished it would continue. He vowed to himself to make them more of a priority, and to stop working so much, and having to go away from them, as soon as he could.

A special delivery package had arrived for Leon at his office, a few days after he had signed the contracts with the General. Inside was Leon's new ID specifying his security clearance level, with the photo he'd used for his passport, even though he'd not given them a copy of that photo.

A chill went down his spine.

How they got hold of that photo he didn't know, but he supposed that the government could do pretty much anything they wanted with their own files. Also inside was a cell phone and charger, with instructions to only use the phone for official business. A sticker on the phone said: "This phone is secured and encrypted." A note from the General told Leon to keep the phone with him and on at all times, as soon a call would be coming that would require him to leave at once for his new job. He was told to ready a travel bag, with enough clothing for a two week stay.

That night, he packed a bag and hid it in the closet, so Mary wouldn't have to look at it; he knew it would only upset her.

During one of their ice cream outings, Leon had bought Jennie and Mary extra-big cones, and they sat outside at the round stone tables of the ice cream shop to eat them. He leaned in to his daughter, "Jennie, daddy's got a new job. I'm not sure when I'm going to start, but it will be soon."

She looked up from her cone, ice cream on the end of her nose. "Are you going to make more money, Daddy?"

He knew where she got thoughts like that from; Mary.

"Yes, I should be. But the bad thing about my new job is that I will have to go away from home sometimes. I will have to stay overnight, maybe for a few days. I'm sorry about that. But I promise you that we'll do something special when I get back home. Ok?"

Jennie nodded. Mary smiled in spite of herself, as Jennie was just too comical with the ice cream on her nose. She took a napkin and wiped Jennie's face.

"Well, that didn't go so bad," Mary said.

He smiled and popped the end of the cone into his mouth. If only his wife was as easy-going as his daughter. He hoped she wouldn't instill too much of her worry about the world into Jennie.

***

Leon was at his office one evening, working late. It was a hard habit for him to break. The office was empty. He was going over some tunnel drawings when the special cell phone rang. He had been carrying it around for weeks, and was starting to think they'd forgotten about him, even though he knew that was highly unlikely. The phone rang again, and then buzzed, vibrating across his desk. His hand went out to grab it, and he hesitated a moment.

Am I sure about this?

He overcame his discomfort and pressed the green button on the phone.

Too late to back out now.

A series of electronic notes played, then the line clicked on.

"Hello? Leon speaking."

"Good evening, sir. There will be a car to pick you up in exactly one hour at your office. Will you be ready, sir?" The voice was a young man's, with an accent from the deep south, obviously having been trained in the military way of speaking.

"Yes, I will be," he answered, feeling the churn of nervous excitement in his stomach, that it was all too real, now. "They are not going to come by my house?"

"No, sir. It will be less noticeable from your office, sir."

"Ah, I see. Yes, I'll be ready."

"Very good, sir. Goodbye."

"Bye."

The caller hung up and the electronic notes played again, this time in reverse. He took the phone away from his ear and looked at the display. It said "Unknown Caller."

He quickly left a note for his secretary that he'd be gone for a few days. He'd told her that a special project was in the works that would require him to travel, and that the call to leave could come at any time. That was as much detail as he went into, but he was not worried about leaving the office in Nancy's hands. She was very capable, and he had gone on numerous business trips in the past with her at the helm. He made a mental note to give her a raise when he got back; he would be able to well afford it.

He drove the short distance to his home quickly and told Mary that he had to leave. She was not happy about it, but he'd given her enough time in advance to deal with it, so she didn't give him much hassle, just some sad looks.

He pulled his nearly-packed bag from the closet and checked that he had everything; all he needed to pack was his shaving kit and tooth brush. The last minute preparing done, he yanked up the handle on the case and started to pull it down the hall.

Pausing outside of Jennie's door, he opened it a crack to look in on her. She was fast asleep in bed, the half-moon nightlight casting a warm, yellow glow on her face. He smiled to himself. He would have liked to hug and kiss her goodbye, but knew it would upset her if she knew he was leaving. So, he pulled the door closed and let her be.

As he made his way downstairs, he was dreading that Mary would create a scene. Instead, she was waiting with a small gift bag for him. Inside were a couple of gourmet, organic, fair trade chocolate bars, a canned coffee, and the latest issue of the gemstone magazine he liked to read.

"Good luck," she said and handed him the bag.

"Aw, thanks. That's really nice of you," he hugged her, then gave her a big kiss.

"I figured you might have a long journey ahead of you, not that I know where you are going..."

"I don't even know where I'm going! Even if I did, you know I couldn't say. I'll make it all up to you and Jennie, I promise."

She put her finger on his lips, then kissed him. "It's ok. I know. Be safe. Will you be able to call me?"

"I think so. I mean, I'm not sure, but I will if I can."

"Ok, hon."

He hugged her again then picked up his suitcase. "I'll talk to you soon."

"Good luck. I love you."

"I love you, too." He tried to smile, though his sadness was showing.

She watched him go out the door and down the driveway to his black SUV, parked next to her identical white one. He put the case in the back, then waved to her before he got in and drove away. Standing on the porch, she felt small and alone. Just before she went in, she caught a glimpse of the light in Jennie's room on the second floor shutting off.

Leon got back to his office in record time, wheeled into his parking space and killed the engine. He sat in silence, his thoughts racing. Due to his nerves, his forehead and armpits were sweaty, and he got out of the car to take off his jacket.

Do I even need a jacket where I'm going? Maybe I'll need a parka?

He got the suitcase out of the back and locked up his car.

Checking his watch, he saw it was exactly an hour since he'd received the phone call. Just then, a black limo with tinted windows pulled into the parking lot and stopped right by him. The driver's door opened and a young man in a black suit stepped out.

"Good evening, sir. I'll take that for you," said the man. It was the same voice Leon had heard on the phone. He took the suitcase and put it in the trunk. The back window of the car rolled down to reveal the face of the General.

"Hello, Leon. How are you doing?" the General asked.

"Very well. Thanks."

"Good. Well, get in and we'll get underway."

The man opened the opposite rear door for Leon. He stepped around the car and peered inside and saw an empty seat next to the General. The car was plush, all soft leather, very cozy inside, and fully decked out. He climbed in and the man closed the door behind him.

The General smiled and shook his hand. "I'm glad you could make it."

Leon was a mess of twisted guts inside; he didn't know what to say. "Thanks," was all he could weakly mutter.

As the limo moved off, the General opened a cigar box and offered it to him. "They're from Cuba, but you didn't hear it from me!" He grinned and slapped Leon on the arm.

He grinned back, and looked over the fat cigars. He took one out, and the General handed him a cutter. They cut the ends of their cigars and lit up. The car also had a bar, and they made themselves drinks. The driver never looked back in the rear-view mirror at them once. There was a clear glass partition between them and the driver, blocking out all sound.

"We've got a few hours to drive, and you won't be living large like this on the base, so enjoy this while you can," the General said, blowing smoke out and taking a sip of whiskey. Leon did enjoy it.

If this is any indication of how I'm going to be treated in my new job, then I'm going to enjoy it very much indeed!

Still, there was a nervousness in his body that the booze couldn't touch, and every once in a while it spiked up into fear, from the depths of his mind.

The General touched a button and the windows in the back of the car changed to totally black, including the partition. They could see nothing outside. "Security procedure," he said, and puffed on his cigar.

4

Leon sat back in the limo and tried to enjoy the ride, even though he was beginning to feel like a prisoner in a plush cage. The car had a great air filtration system and the cigars didn't cloud up the back of the limo, even with the windows closed. In awe of the engineering, he tried to contain his excitement; the further wonders he was about to experience as a military insider would blow his socks off, he expected.

The General was quiet for most of the trip. He was friendly enough, answering whatever questions Leon put to him as best he could, at least questions that didn't require answers above Leon's security clearance level; of these there were many.

Mostly though, the General smoked his cigars and watched the news on a small TV screen. He had recruited hundreds of civilians into secret military service, and the thrill was mostly gone for him. "I wish I was going where you are, get right in the action! It's always exciting down there," the General said, flipping through the channels.

"Excitement is something I like to avoid underground. Any action down there that we don't create is bad news, and is probably a cave-in, or seismic activity. We try to plan for any surprises."

The General scoffed and laughed a little to himself. "That's not what I was meaning, Leon. I've been down there many times and

I well know the risks. I was referring to the Greys and doing something to stop them. You read the briefing papers, they were in there."

"You're telling me that stuff was real? Not just some cover story to lure people into military service? My "patriotic duty" and all? I thought maybe you were giving me something to hang my hat on about saving the world, if I needed that."

The General looked him straight in the eyes, with a gaze that could cut stone, "Afraid not. This is serious stuff. The aliens are real, and have been visiting us for some time. A long time, in fact. They have been getting more aggressive in their dealings with us. Seems they don't like our underground bases that much. They feel we're intruding on their territory."

"*Their* territory? Assuming they exist – which I won't be able to believe until I actually see some with my own eyes, sorry. How is the Earth, or anything under the Earth's surface part of *their* territory?"

The General filled up his whiskey glass again and added ice cubes. "Well..." he slowly trailed off, and then took a big drink.

He's drunk enough to be wasted by now, but he's not showing any signs of it. The man can hold his liquor!

The General lowered his glass, "There are some theories that the ETs are actually our creators, that they came to Earth a long, long time ago, and made us by taking DNA from ape-men and changing it to make us Homosapiens. Now, I don't know whether *that's* true or not, but I do know that the Greys are here and are living underground, among other places."

"The aliens have underground bases?"

"D.U.M.B.s? Yep."

"I see."

"You are familiar with the term, I take it? How could you not be, being a professional underground engineer?"

"I'm familiar, of course: Deep Underground Military Bases. But you're sure about this? It's wild to contemplate." He tried to keep his composure, and picked his words carefully. He wanted to say to the General that what he was saying was crazy, but that was not a good move with your new boss. Yet, it's how he felt.

The General laughed, a little cackling laugh, "You better believe it! Those sons-of-bitches have been down there for a lot longer that we have! They've got tunnels running all over the damn place! The hardest thing for us when we want to make a new base is not the actual construction; that's a snap these days. No, it's finding a place where we don't run over one of their bases, or tunnels, or encounter them while we're down there. They have proven to get nasty when they're cornered. Goddamn bugs!" He gulped his drink and his face become twisted up and bitter.

Leon could tell there was a lot more he wanted say about the aliens, but it looked like it was only going to upset him further. The General's hatred of the aliens frightened Leon and made him question, again, whether he'd done the right thing by getting involved with the whole secret military operation.

But really, I didn't have a choice!

Yes you did — you could have said no and watched your life fall apart. Or, killed yourself...

It was too late for him now, he knew, and he'd just have to ride it out. He poured himself another vodka and orange juice (heavy on the vodka), and sipped it as he stared at the TV at some inane show, feeling the numbing warmth spread over his body.

The General spoke again, after a few minutes of the TV filling the silence, calmer now, "Yeah, those cockroaches are not our friends, I'll tell you that. But it's not all bad. We've gotten a lot of technology from salvaging their wrecks. They like to keep to themselves for the most part, but they do abduct people sometimes. Not much we can do to stop that, yet. But if you ever find one underground, shoot first and ask questions later, I'll tell you that much! You'll be issued a sidearm when you get to the base. Carry it at all times when you are on operations. And, watch your back."

***

Hours later, the limo turned off the main highway and continued down a dirt road marked "Private. No trespassing."

Leon and the General had been nodding off during the long drive, due to traveling through the night and the booze, but the sudden slowing of motion made them wake up, even though they could not see out the windows.

There was an automatic gate that rose as they approached, triggered by a sensor in the limo. The long car went down the dirt road for several miles, passing cameras, heat sensors, and motion detectors; their every move monitored and recorded.

Finally, the limo pulled up to a large second gate, with razor wire on the top, and a guard booth staffed with armed soldiers in green-brown, digital camouflage pattern uniforms. The patches on their shoulders depicted cartoonish dwarfs with long beards, holding picks and large hammers, surrounded by a ring of stars and the words "Diggers 18th" in gold thread on a black background. They wore no other identifying marks, nor any flags.

The driver stopped at the gate and lowered his window to speak to the guard. The driver seemed to know the guard, but still handed over his ID, which the guard swiped into a hand-held card reader. The guard then took another device from his belt and held it up to the driver's eyes to scan his retinas.

Then, the guard moved to the back door of the limo as the General rolled down the window. Through the open window, Leon could see that the sky was starting to lighten up as dawn approached; they'd been driving all night.

The guard saluted, "Good morning, General."

"Thank you," the General returned the salute. He produced his ID for the guard, and then had his eyes scanned, too. The General gestured at Leon, "He's new, but he's got a temporary ID."

"No problem," said the guard, stepping over to Leon's window. "Can I see your ID for a moment?"

Leon handed over his ID card and it was read by the machine.

The guard passed his card back. "Have you ever had a retina scan?"

Leon shook his head.

"Well, there's nothing to it, and it doesn't hurt a bit. It won't hurt your eyes either. Just look at the X and keep still until I tell you," the guard raised the eye scanner in front of Leon's eyes. A green light shot out of the scanner and moved over his eyeballs. He didn't feel anything. Within a few seconds the device beeped and the guard lowered it.

"There we go. We've got a new base-line reading for you. The next time it will be even faster. Thank you, gentlemen." The guard saluted and stepped back to his post. The General saluted back, then raised the blacked-out window.

The gate opened and the limo crept down a long, winding paved road to a few rounded metal buildings of various sizes, painted dark green, set within a ring of hills. The largest building was as big as an aircraft hanger and could easily fit a commercial jetliner inside. There was an airstrip behind the buildings, but no planes were in sight.

The General switched the windows back to clear. Leon gazed out with interest, taking it all in, as the General sat back, puffing away.

The General announced, "Welcome to Greyland. This place doesn't exist. Even if it did exist I couldn't talk about it," he winked.

The limo pulled to a stop in front of the main building and they got out, stretching their limbs. The sun was just starting to rise above the hills and the air was still. The base looked rundown, and not at all what Leon had been imagining.

"This is it? That's all?" he turned around in a circle.

"That's all. At least for the topside attractions. The real action is down under, as you'd expect. Come on." The General clapped him on the back and they walked in, passing through a very thick door, with concrete rising on either side.

"That was a long drive. How come we didn't fly here?"

"We like to keep a low profile. We only fly in and out of here when it's absolutely necessary."

Inside, it was as drab as the outside; with olive green walls and fluorescent lighting. A secretary came to meet them, a young blonde woman with short hair and a fit body, wearing the same uniform that the guards outside wore. Leon looked at the patches on her uniform, intrigued by their symbolism.

She saluted, "Good morning, General Simpson. And, your visitor. Welcome."

"Thank you, Sergeant," the General returned the salute. "This is Leon Verdat. He's a civilian contractor with 15 above Top Secret clearance, a specialist in underground tunnel boring and construction. He'll be based out of here for the time being."

"Very good, General. I'll see to it that he settles in just fine."

"Good, good. Got any coffee ready?" The General stepped further into the office, looking around for the coffee pot.

"There should be some on, in the kitchen" She extended her hand to Leon. "I'm Cathy Peterson, the go-to girl on the base. Anything the contractors need, they just ask me. So, feel free."

Leon shook her hand. "Thanks. Any chance I can make a phone call to my wife?"

The General waved Leon into a conference room. "Over here!"

"I guess I'll do it later!"

Leon trudged along the hallway, feeling exhaustion in his bones.

Once inside the room, the General handed him a cup of coffee. "I know you must be tired. I am too. I'll make this as brief as I can, then we can both get some rest. Sorry for the night traveling, but that's what the schedule dictated." He then shut the door and turned on a video projector connected to a strange-looking laptop.

The projector came to life, throwing light onto a screen at the front of the room. The General took him through a presentation that consisted of maps of the underground base, engineering diagrams, blueprints, and photos; all in greater detail than Leon had previously been told. He clicked through the screens as he spoke.

"The facility you are in now dates back to the 1940's. It was commissioned soon after the Roswell crash in New Mexico." He showed Leon black and white photos and newspaper clippings from the UFO crash in 1947, in Roswell, New Mexico. "The

Roswell crash was one of the most publicized UFO crashes ever, but it was not the only one, not by a long shot! You've probably heard of it. Well, let me tell you, it was real. Public interest in Roswell continues to this day, and we've had to do a lot to encourage people to leave it alone, though that doesn't seem to be working. There is a lot more interesting and compelling evidence of ETs out there, but most people are looking in the wrong place: up instead of down."

He displayed the next screens, showing pictures of the Roswell crash that no member of the public had ever seen: close-up shots of unmistakable aliens, clear images of parts of a UFO, and even a live, Grey alien in custody.

Leon put his hand over his mouth, out of shock, "There were real aliens found? Alive?"

"Not alive for long, but yes." The General laughed. "Leon, you've got to get over it, aliens are real! And, they are here, I'm telling you!"

"It's not that I don't want to believe you, or think you're not telling me the truth, but until I..."

"Until you see it for yourself. I know. I was the same as you. Ok, let's go see one, then. How about that?"

"Sure, if you've got any on ice, or anything!" Leon joked.

The General closed the laptop, then stood up. "Come on." He walked from the room. Leon followed, slowly, nervous, "Where are we going?"

They passed a few offices, all filled with soldiers working away on computers. The lights were too bright after being in the darkened conference room. Leon blinked profusely and rubbed his tired eyes.

"The freezer in the hanger," said the General, lighting up a cigar.

"You can smoke in here? I'm surprised."

"Not supposed to. But I'm the high ranking officer here right now!" The General smiled, then puffed a big bunch of smoke out that swirled in the air.

They came to a heavy, steel reinforced door with an iris scanner, a place to swipe an ID card, and a keypad.

"Hello," said a computerized voice from a speaker on the door. "Please look into the iris scanner to verify your identity."

The General put his face near the scanner and let his eyes be read.

"Thank you, General Simpson. Now, insert you ID card into the slot below."

He unclipped his ID card from the front pocket of his shirt and put it in the reader.

The computer beeped. "Thank you. Now, please enter your access code on the keypad."

The General did this, shielding the keypad with his hand so Leon could not see.

"It's not that I don't trust you...but I don't trust you," the General winked. "Besides, it's procedure." He nodded at the camera on the wall, recording their every move.

Leon shrugged.

"Thank you, General. Access is granted for you and your guest."

Leon looked at the speaker, then at the camera. "How does it know?"

"Visual recognition. Audio recognition. Plus, a weight sensor in the floor. It knows my weight, so there must be someone with me. There's probably other kinds of sensors, too, I'd bet on it."

"Like what?"

"Oh, something that examines the air. Maybe a heat-sensing camera. Any number of things."

The locks on the heavy door popped open and air hissed out. Then, the door started to swing out, slowly.

"Please remove your ID card," the computer reminded him.

The General pulled his card out of the reader and clipped it back onto his pocket.

Once the door had opened enough, the General stepped inside and Leon followed.

Leon was immediately shocked by the size of the room he'd just stepped into; it was a massive hanger, built into the hillside behind the building. Sections of the floor were large square cutouts, which were elevators with jet fighters on them; they moved up and down, ferrying planes and gear, to and from the levels underneath. There were a number of men practicing their martial arts moves in metal exoskeletons in one area, helicopters being worked on in another, and small flying vehicles of various types that he had never seen before; ultralights and experimental craft, across the vast floor.

"Wow!" He blinked and tried to take it all in, but it was too much for a glance.

"Come on, I'll show you around. Watch the door."

The door behind them started to beep and then closed itself, sealing up the entrance again, with the airlock hissing. The General walked deeper inside and shook hands with a mechanic that was tending to one of the planes. Leon tried to watch where he was walking, as there were cables and hazards on the floor, but the sights were taking his attention and he stubbed his toes, often.

"This here's Leon. He's going to be working with us, from the civilian side. Make sure you treat him right."

The mechanic held his hand out to Leon. "I sure will, General. The name's Jim, pleased to meet you."

Leon shook the man's hand. "Likewise. Jim."

"Come on, Leon," the General walked ahead, puffing on his stogie, trailing smoke.

He led him into a room, then down a flight of stairs, and through another set of doors, for which he had to swipe his ID card. Cameras watched their every move and Leon glanced at them with suspicion.

They are probably listening to us too, and scanning us with microwaves and infrared, God knows what!

They continued on until the General stopped in front of a room with two armed guards posted outside it, that looked like the entrance to a bank vault, with a solid, thick, air-locked metal door.

"What is this, Fort Knox?" Leon quipped.

"More valuable," the General exhaled a thick cloud of smoke that mixed in the overhead lights. "How goes, boys?" he saluted the men.

"Hello, General, sir!" the first guard saluted.

"Doing good, General. Thank you, sir!" the second guard saluted.

"I'm giving Leon here the tour."

"Very good, sir," the first guard picked up an iris scanner and held it in front of the General, who positioned his eyes in front of it. The device scanned his eyes and beeped.

The General handed his ID card over and the second soldier scanned it into a reader, which also beeped, then he handed it back. Next, the guard handed the reader over so the General could enter a code. The device then beeped. The lock on the metal door clicked open.

"Thank you, sir," the first guard said, and held the door for them.

A blast of cool air shot out, chilling them instantly.

"Thank you, boys," the General dropped the stub of his cigar into a metal trash can. He ventured inside and took a few steps down a short hallway, then turned back to Leon. "Come on in. There's jackets if you need one," he pointed to the parkas that hung on the wall.

At the end of the short hallway was a doorway hung with jiggling, clear plastic partitions on the frame, making it look like the entrance to a commercial walk-in freezer.

Or, a morgue.

The guards shut the door behind them, and the locks clicked back into place. The airlock resealed.

Leon tried to push any thoughts of morgues and dead bodies away. "What, are we gonna make something to eat?"

"There's no food in here, unless you like meat from another planet." The General pushed the plastic slats to the side and stepped in.

Leon followed him into a metal room, lit with florescent tubes on the ceiling, and looking every bit like a morgue; with metal tables, sinks, surgical-type equipment, and large drawers set into one wall. It was below freezing in there, as evidenced by the thermometer on the wall, and their visible breath.

The General went over to the wall with the drawers.

Just like the morgues in TV shows.

"This is just a PR freezer, you could call it. We keep a sample here to show any visitors that might pass this way with a need to know and the proper security clearance. The real good stuff is hidden far underground, in several very secure locations. But this does fine to put to rest the curiosity of most doubters we have to work with. It's also good for getting us extra funding when we show this to certain politicians," he grinned.

Grabbing the handle of a drawer, he pulled it out to reveal the outline of a small body in a black, plastic body bag. It could have been a child, except it had a very large head.

Just like the aliens have...

Leon felt his mouth go dry and it was suddenly hard to swallow.

This can't be real...

The General grabbed the zipper of the bag and held it.

"I think it's important that you see this, so you know what we're up against. Ready? Once you see this, there's no going back. Your whole idea of the world as you know it is going to change."

"It's been changing already, so what's a bit more excitement?"

"Good attitude." He pulled down the zipper to reveal a dead Grey alien body.

A foul stench hit them.

"Oh, my God..."

"Sorry, I forgot to warn you about the stink," the General smiled and put his hand over his nose.

Leon didn't think he'd really forgotten, however. He covered his nose with his sleeve as an acidic smell, like very strong rotting fruit, met his nose. "Gah!"

He looked down at the dead alien; a Grey, with winkled, greyish skin, a small mouth, tiny holes for a nose, and large, oval eyes, which were closed. It had no ears he could see and the mouth was open in a grimace. It had some cuts on its body. It looked like it had taken some abuse before it died.

"We recovered this one in a crash a few years back. He didn't live long, as he was too injured from the impact. I say "he" but there doesn't appear to be any sex organs, so I don't know what it really is. Our troops shot its ship down over the mountains, not far from here."

"Does this kind of thing happen often? Shooting down their ships?"

"More than you'd believe. Most of the time people never even see them. Very few people bother to look up these days, being too busy on their phones and such. Plus, the aliens have some pretty good cloaking devices. Usually, their ships are invisible to the naked eye, and even invisible to our radar, unless they want us to see them. We have to use special radar arrays to detect their ships when the cloaking is on, and even those don't always work."

Leon moved closer to the body, as close as he dared without touching it. He wanted to touch it, to make sure it was real, but he was nervous to touch it, in case he contracted a disease.

"You can touch it. It's been sterilized. Besides, they don't really carry much in the way of diseases. They've got advanced tech as you would imagine, for hygiene on their ships, and protection from diseases. Doesn't seem to help with the stink much. Dunno why."

Leon reached out his hand, and slowly, carefully touched the alien's head with his finger. It was like touching a frozen piece of meat. There were tiny black hairs on its head, almost too small to see. He wondered if the alien had a family; parents, brothers, sisters. Or, maybe it was just a clone, as he'd seen in movies and heard in other stories. The briefing documents had said they were likely clones, though seeing one up close, even dead, he found it hard to believe it was real, never mind a clone; that was a whole other level he was still wrapping his head around.

"How many of them have you found?"

"In that crash, a couple. There are usually between two and five to an average ship. Many more on a larger vessel."

"And, since Roswell? How many have you found, or captured, in total?"

The General looked him over, not saying anything for a moment, then: "I'm not at liberty to divulge the exact number, but I can tell you there have been hundreds of known crashes over the decades; not that the public knows about them, of course. Sometimes we'll find a hive underground with dozens, even hundreds of them."

"Hive? So, they share a group mind?"

The General zipped up the bag and pushed the drawer back into place with a solid clunking sound. Then, he made his way to the door. They were both starting to shiver with the cold and their breath was coming out in ragged puffs.

"Most of them do. As near as we can tell they are mostly clones, though we do get the odd one that is different. Those are usually the commanders, bigger and taller than the rest. We think they're programmed biological robots, just following orders, or they are remotely controlled. We're not sure yet, but we have theories we are pursing. We have found some type of communication waves that they receive and they also beam transmissions back to a source, but we've yet to locate that source."

They stepped out of the morgue, back past the hanging plastic strips, and rubbed their hands, warming up in the more regular room temperature and started walking back down the hallway. The General pushed a button on the wall near the vault-like door and spoke into a speaker there: "We're done."

"Coming, sir," answered one of the guards.

"Get's chilly in there, huh?" The General grinned and fitted another cigar between his lips.

"Y-yeah," Leon rubbed his arms.

One of the soldiers unlocked the door and the air hissed out as he pulled it open.

The General turned to Leon, "So, what do you think, now that you've seen one?"

Leon shook his head, "It's going to take a while to sink in. I think all of this is."

"It can be a lot to take in. Let's get you settled. We'll go down below tomorrow."

"There are tunnels under here?" Leon raised his eyebrows.

"Of course! We're right on top of an entrance point to a main tunnel system. Why do you think I brought you all the way out here? Come on."

The General took him to a supply room. There were rows of weapons and equipment in a large cage. He unlocked the door and they walked in. The General selected a holster and a black handgun; a forty-five caliber, semi-automatic, along with some extra magazines of ammunition in a holster.

"Wear this at all times when you are on the base, from now on." The General handed him the weapon. "Have you shot before?"

"Not since I was a kid, and that was a little twenty-two." He looked at the General's leg and noticed that he carried the same gun in a holster.

"We have a range here. We'll get you up to speed, quick."

The General found a cardboard box marked "Verdat, L." and opened it. Inside were two sets of new, light green-brown, digital camouflage uniforms in Leon's size, a pair of black, leather boots in his size, a helmet in his size with camouflage pattern and attached was a headset, and light, then body armour in the same camo pattern that went over his chest, arms, and legs.

"This is your dress code for the base. I expect you to be in full uniform tomorrow, even if you're not a recruit. Ok?"

"Alright." He accepted the heavy box the General put into his arms, struggling to hold it all up.

"Come on, I'll show you to your "suite.""

The military-issued room the General set him up in was a lot more than what most of the regular recruits got, but it was still sparse; a single bed, a small desk, a functional bathroom, a kitchenette, and a TV. There was a phone plugged into a wall jack, and a strange-looking laptop computer on a small desk, plugged into the power outlet and an Ethernet connection.

The laptop was thick and bulky, with a metal case and rubber corners. It looked like it could take a lot of abuse and was tethered to the desk by a thick security cable.

"You can use the phone and the computer at your discretion; they are both secure and encrypted, and can access military-only resources. The phone will dial numbers here on the base, or to the outside world. The computer will access the public Internet, and also our mil darknet."

"What's that?"

"That's another, secret, secure Internet that can only be accessed via special servers and protocols. It's mostly unknown, and unseen, hence "dark" and unavailable to those not in our group. A Black Ops Intranet, in this case."

"Holy shit! What's on it?" He looked over the laptop, and it was unlike any computer he'd ever seen before; very sturdy and sleek. He couldn't wait to try it.

"Just about everything you could imagine, and a lot of things you couldn't. For your purposes, your computer has been set up to give you access to our engineering database of tunnel boring machines and our current project specs. You can read about the machines we use, any problems we've had with them, and how we fixed them – that type of thing."

"Thanks, that sounds neat!"

"I think you'll find it interesting."

Leon tapped the laptop and smiled, "So, is this thing bulletproof, or what?"

"Of course. Anyway, I thought all that data might come in handy in your work with us. Just use your name and date of birth as the passwords when it asks you, and then give it your biometrics. Now, if you'll excuse me, I have duties to attend to." The General saluted and left the room.

Leon saluted in response, feeling silly doing it, and watched the General walk quickly down the polished tile floor of the hallway.

He shut the door and looked around the room. "Home, sweet home," he sighed and lay down on the bed. Being up all night was taking its toll on him, and aliens or not, before he knew it, he was dozing off.

A short time later, he awoke with a start and sat up, scared, with images of the dead Grey in his head. He took some deep breaths and managed to calm down.

He looked at the time, saw that it was evening, and wondered what Mary and Jennie were doing; a familiar voice would be most welcome. He had his cell phone still, and debated about turning it on. No one had told him to leave it behind, or not to use it. He turned it on and waited for the phone to register on the network. The screen just said "Unable to connect," so he shut it off.

"Must have cell phone blockers." He picked up the phone on the desk and dialed his home number. It seemed to ring for an eternity before she picked up.

"Hello? Leon?"

"Hi. It's me."

"Oh, it's good to hear your voice! Are you ok?"

"Yeah," he wiped his forehead. He wanted to sleep. "We drove all night, and...well, I'm here. That's about all I can really say, I guess." He closed his eyes, but images of the dead alien jolted him, again.

She was silent for a moment. "Well, I'm just glad to hear you arrived safely."

"Thanks, me too. Is Jennie still awake? I'll say hi to her if you put her on."

"Sure, just a sec."

There was a slight pause as she took the phone to their daughter, many hundreds of miles way, in a seemingly different world from the one he now found himself in. Then, his daughter came on the line, full of excitement.

"Daddy, daddy! Where are you?"

"I'm away for work. I just wanted to tell you to be a good girl for your mother while I'm gone."

"I will be, daddy."

"Alright, then.

"Are you coming home, daddy?"

"Not for a while, yet. Not for a while."

"Please, hurry up!"

He grinned. "I will. Go get ready for bed now, and put your mother back on."

Ok, daddy, we miss you!"

"I miss you, too. Now, go to bed, and have a good night."

"I will. I love you, daddy."

"I love you, too."

41

Mary came back on the line. "She's taking it very well. Better than me. She really misses you. I do, too."

He sighed. He'd only been gone a short time and hoped this assignment wasn't going to be too hard on his family. "I miss you both very much, and I'll be back as soon as I can. Until then, try not to worry. Ok?" He gripped the phone tighter. He'd been away before on civilian assignments, but it was never easy with a young child, and he found this time was particularity difficult. He felt a wave of loneliness sweep through him.

There was a pause in her response. "I hope so..."

"Haven't I always come home safe from jobs before?"

"Yes, but you've never worked a job like *this* before."

He watched the sun setting out of the small window. He leaned back in the chair and wished she was with him now. He had a sudden desire to make love to her on the small bed in his room, as visions of hotel rooms they had stayed in on vacations came to mind.

"I'll be extra careful, and I'll be home soon, I promise."

"I hope so."

"It's been a long day. I'm gonna turn in. I'll call you tomorrow, ok?"

"Take extra good care."

"I will."

"Goodbye. Stay safe. I love you."

"I love you, too. Good night."

Hanging up the phone and finding himself alone in that room, on the base, was about the most lonely feeling he could imagine. It was one of the hardest phone calls he had ever made.

He looked at the laptop and his curiosity got to him. The case was all metal, ribbed, and reinforced, with thick rubber stoppers on the corners to protect it from impacts. It was heavy and felt very solid. There was a carrying case for the laptop on the floor, with an instruction manual inside it. Flipping through the manual, he found out that the laptop was waterproof, dustproof, vibrationproof, shockproof, crushproof, EMFproof, and bulletproof against many common calibers of bullets.

He whistled, "Wonder how much *this* cost to develop?"

He opened the laptop and the screen came to life. It was an operating system like he'd never seen before, of military design.

A box on the screen blinked: "Enter your full name."

He typed it in and another box appeared: "Enter your date of birth." He entered that too, then the computer prompted him to: "Place your thumb on the fingerprint reader."

"Fingerprint reader?"

Looking at the side of the computer, he found a small, round disc made of smooth, transparent material. He put his finger on the disc and it lit up.

"Scanning," a box on the screen read.

Then, the screen blinked: "Calibration Successful" and let him into the system.

Where did they get my fingerprint from, to check against? I didn't give any prints to the military.

He had no arrest record with the police, so the only thing he could think of was that the Department of Motor Vehicles had his thumb print. Thinking that they might have shared it with the military gave him goose bumps.

Tired, but feeling unable to sleep (every time he closed his eyes he saw the dead Grey in the freezer), he spent the rest of the evening poking around the limited databases that were available to him. He found it fascinating to read through the plans of the tunnel boring machines and reports on them. Mostly, they were like the machines he'd used in his civilian life as a contractor for large construction projects, but he came across some very interesting modifications to the machinery that made them much more efficient and effective. But there were features of the machines that he could retrieve no data about.

Also, when he tried to access any plans, or maps of the tunnels, he was met with "Access Denied" on the screen.

So, they want me to work on their project, but they don't trust me enough to see the layout of the tunnels?

It was to be expected that some material would be off-limits to him, so he shrugged it off – it was the military, after all. And, a secret one at that!

Compartmentalization. Figures.

He stretched, then got up from the computer and stretched some more. Then, he yawned. It had been a long day.

He took a hot shower, which relaxed him some, but still the images of the dead Grey would not leave his mind.

He went to bed, but sleep was hard to come by, and when it did, he had nightmares of Greys.

5

The next morning he was roused by knocking on his door.

"Mister Verdat. Time to rise and shine. It's 6AM," the voice beyond the door was that of the woman he had met when he first arrived.

What was her name? Cathy? Sergeant something?

"I'm up, I'm up," he scrambled to get to the door. "Hold on a sec!" He opened the door just a bit, hiding behind it, as he was in his undies.

"Good morning!" She was freshly dressed for the day and smiled wide, revealing perfect, white teeth.

She's probably been up for a while, and had a run, or something, already.

"Good morning," he mumbled, with sleep-thick lips.

"Breakfast will be served in a half-hour, and you're meeting with General Simpson. Coffee and juice is available now in the kitchen. Please help yourself." She saluted him and walked away.

"Thanks," he quickly saluted her back, but he was going to have to anticipate it next time and pick up his speed, as he had missed her.

What's with all this saluting stuff, anyway? Jeez!

He guessed it was just a force of habit with the career military people to salute each other. But it was also a sign of respect, after all, he knew.

He showered and dressed quickly. He'd never seen himself in a military uniform before, and he watched himself in the mirror as he did up the last buttons on his tunic. He scrunched up his face.

"GI fuckin' Joe!"

He sighed.

Relax! It's only for a little while; think of how much they're paying you!

The brand new boots fit and were comfortable, even though he turned his feet this way and that, trying to get used to the look of them.

Once dressed in his new, stiff clothes, he made his way to the kitchen for some coffee. He'd gotten halfway down the hallway before he remembered that he was supposed to wear his handgun at all times while on the base.

He quickly went back to his room and dug out his gun; it was in his bag of clothes, where he'd hidden it for safekeeping. He strapped it on and was struck by how much it weighed, as it sagged down on his leg. He made a mental note to get some time on the shooting range so he could get used to it, then went to go meet the General.

He stopped again and looked at the body armour laying on the floor.

"Ah, shit!"

***

He tromped down the hallway, struggling under the weight of the full uniform, with the helmet, boots, body armour, rifle, handgun, and belt with many pouches on it. He felt a bit strange wearing all the gear topside, but it was what had been asked of him. Still, he was somewhat glad for an opportunity to try it all out again, as he wanted to get used to wearing it; it might just save his life next time. The farther he walked, the heavier it all seemed to get, and he hadn't even had any coffee, yet.

Goddammit!

The General was waiting for him at table in the canteen, munching on a big breakfast of bacon, eggs, hash browns, toast, coffee, and orange juice. He smiled a little to see the General in his camouflage uniform, too.

Now we're all dressed the same. I feel like I'm in high school with the uniforms again. But where's his armour?

He looked around the room at the soldiers at the tables and none of them had their body armour on.

"A bit overdressed for breakfast, aren't we, Verdat?" the General chuckled and wiped his mouth.

"Ah, dammit!" Leon sat down heavily at the table and started taking off the armour plates.

"No, leave it on! I want to get a picture!" The General pulled out his phone and started snapping shots.

"Please, don't! I feel stupid enough already!"

"Nonsense! It happens to the greenhorns quite a bit. Seems a lot of you newbies can't tell the difference between "full uniform" and "battle dress!"

The other soldiers had turned to stare. Several were laughing out loud and taking pictures.

"The ribbing will die down...eventually!" the General grinned and went back to eating. "How did you sleep?"

"Fine," Leon pouted.

"That's good. Many have a had time relaxing at a place like this, especially after seeing a real, dead alien."

He shrugged, "I guess I was just tired from the excitement of the trip and all." He let the chest plate clunk to the floor, then pulled off his helmet, arm and leg armours, putting them in a pile.

Soldiers stopped by to get pictures of the pile of gear.

"Ah, come, on!" Leon shooed them away. "Look, maybe I don't belong here." He stood up.

The General narrowed his eyes at the troops taking pictures, "Ok, that's enough, now. Let us eat in peace."

The troops went back to their respective tables, but the occasional burst of laughter still broke out.

Leon got himself a tray, piled it up with food and sat back down opposite the General.

A few day workers in civilian clothes had arrived and looked Leon over, but didn't stare long, as he was with the General.

The General nodded at them, "Those folks are technology specialists that have been working with us for a while. They're civilians too, locals. Working at the base is their day job."

"Cool. Wish I could go home too, at the end of the day."

"You might be able to, in time. Maybe things will work out for you with us, and you can move closer."

"Maybe, but where are *their* uniforms? I don't see them carrying around all this shit!"

"Easy, Leon. They're going to get changed, too."

"Ok, good."

A laugh came from across the room.

"By the way, "full uniform" just means your boots, fatigues, and your sidearm. The rest is for when we are on operations."

"Now you tell me!"

"I thought it would have been obvious."

"I guess I don't watch enough military movies." He slugged back some orange juice and chased it with coffee.

The General grinned, then slid a paper napkin between them. He took out a pen and started to sketch. "As I mentioned before, this base is over a tunnel. Actually, a tunnel system connects under here. We've been working on a new tunnel, to extend the network, but we've run into some snags and have had to halt construction, temporally."

He peered over his plate as the General drew. "What snags?"

"We've been having trouble chewing through a particularly tough strain of bedrock. It's been breaking all of our bits."

"I've seen that sort of thing before. I'm sure there's something I can do."

"With the bits, I've no doubt. But there's more. That's only the first problem."

"Oh?'

"The tunnel we are making now is to join up with an existing tunnel that connects to the maglev system coming from another tunnel to the east."

"Maglev?"

The General sighed. "I'm going to have to go over a lot with you, aren't I?"

Leon shrugged, "I dunno. I'm a civilian, after all! I've heard some rumors about what you've been doing down there, but how do I know what's truth and fiction? I just saw a real, dead alien body last night. Give a guy a break!"

The General smiled, "I do tend to take for granted the things I know. I've seen a lot of things that most people never will. Sometimes that's good; other times not. I have nightmares."

"I'll bet."

"The tunnel we are making is only about a quarter complete." He moved his pen over the napkin, tracing the lines of the tunnels he had drawn. "Once we get to about fifty percent, we should be able to link up with the other maglev line."

"You still haven't told me what that is."

"The maglev? Wasn't it in your briefing materials? Hmm, probably not. Well, it's a monorail system that rides on magnets. It's very quiet, very comfortable, energy efficient, and fast. It's been clocked up to near the speed of sound."

"But the speed of sound is what? Over seven hundred miles per hour?"

"Seven hundred and sixty-eight. But we dare not go over that, as we'd rather not produce sonic booms underground. That might raise too much attention. We only do so when it's an emergency."

"Naturally. Sounds amazing. How extensive is this line?"

"Thousands of miles. These maglev lines go all over the Earth. We have our own line, the Russians have theirs, the Chinese are building one. Who knows who else by now; there are many private firms and corporations with the means, and the desire to go underground these days. And, of course the Greys have theirs."

"The aliens have a maglev line, too? Will wonders never cease?"

"Yes. I'm not sure how they started it. They've had bases underground for longer than we have. It was a surprise, to say the least, when we first built our tunnels and found theirs already in place!" He shoved the napkin out of the way and picked up a piece of toast to chew on.

"Wow," Leon ran his fingers through his hair. "This is so much to take in. I think my head is spinning."

"You get used to it. All done eating?"

The General took him back into the hanger and down a hallway they had not ventured before. It was lit by safety lights and had warning signs that said they were entering a "restricted area." They went through a blast door that the General unlocked with his ID badge, code, and biometric eye scan. Once through the door, the floor sloped down at a steep angle. By the end of it they were several meters under the surface. This started to get Leon excited, as they were now underground.

There were two armed soldiers at the end of the hallway who saluted when the General passed by. The hallway ended in a door with yellow caution markings on it. There was another iris scan to give, a code to enter, and a place to swipe the General's ID card. The General went through this near-ritual and the door unlocked with a hiss of air as its airlock was broken, revealing an elevator.

"This is the way down." The General walked aboard.

It was like no elevator car Leon had ever seen; it had a dozen seats in it, similar to car seats, with safety belts. The General sat down and strapped himself in. Leon watched him, then decided he'd better follow along, so he did likewise.

The General touched a small screen on the arm of his chair and entered some commands. The door of the elevator closed and then it started to move, very quickly down.

Leon felt his stomach lurch, like the drop of a roller-coaster. "Woah!" He grabbed the arms of his chair.

The General grinned. He always liked to see the reactions of the newbies to one of the fastest, deepest elevators on the planet.

"Fun, huh? Two miles, straight down, at a hundred miles an hour!"

"It's wild, alright!" Leon raised his voice over the noise.

"One of the best rides in any amusement park! We can go faster, too," the General explained over the whining noise, "in an emergency, this thing can get up to three hundred miles per hour!"

"Unreal!" He sat back in his chair, starting to get used to the movement.

Then, within a couple of minutes, the elevator came smoothly to a stop. The door opened and warm air rushed in, with a tinge of damp and dirt in it; Leon knew at once they were deep underground. The General unbuckled and stepped out into another hallway. Leon followed, but he was not very graceful on shaky legs.

They entered what looked like a military version of a modern subway platform, carved out of deep, solid rock. It was part natural cave, and part excavation that had been converted to a maglev station. There were even some stalagmites and stalactites left at the far ends of the platform.

"It's the Batcave!" Leon goofed.

"Except this one's real."

There were two monorail lines running in opposite directions, with a concrete island in the middle, connected by walkways. Several more armed soldiers were on the platform, to each side. They saluted the General as they passed by.

Leon went to the bare rock wall and touched it, marveling at the construction, feeling his love for the dirt stirring him, again. It was warm. "We must be very deep, I'm feeling geothermal heating starting already in this strata."

"Yes, about two miles. Cooling is an ongoing issue for us, and it gets worse the deeper we go."

"Strange how that happens, isn't it? You'd expect just the opposite."

"Until you hit the molten core of the Earth, then you'd damn well know where it was coming from."

"That's still just a theory. You know anyone who's actually been there?"

"Can't say I do. That doesn't mean some haven't reached it."

Leon turned in circles, looking up at the vaulted ceiling hewed out of sold rock. "This is amazing! You've got your own subway system down here!"

"Maglev."

"Right, maglev. But wow! How old is this place? It looks new."

"I'm not at liberty to say."

"Ah."

Multiple, large LCD displays showed that the next train was due to arrive in one minute, from the origin point of "S3" and going to the destination of "S4." A computerized, female voice spoke out the information about the arriving train, and it echoed in the cathedral-like station.

"Don't touch anything," the General warned, as they passed by a control console with many buttons.

"I wouldn't dream of it," Leon continued craning his neck around to take everything in.

They went down a metal staircase to the main platform below.

"You're in luck. The next 'lev is due now," the General nodded in the direction of the blowing air from the tunnel.

"Who's on it? Can we go for a ride?"

"I'm not sure who's on it, off the top of my head, but I could find out easily enough if I wanted to. And yes, we'll be taking a ride."

The air continued to swirl around them and the pressure increased. The soldiers stepped back from the edge of the platform and took a better grip on their weapons.

"Expecting trouble?" He looked at the General, his brow furrowed.

"No, it's just procedure for the guards to look lively when a 'lev arrives. You never know when trouble will strike down here, so it's better to expect it than to be caught unaware. Though, if anything had happened, then the alarms would have gone off. That's assuming someone had time to trigger them. I've learned not to rely on those, either." The General pulled his handgun out of its holster.

Leon touched the holster at his side and tentatively pulled out his handgun, too.

What the hell? Just in case.

He looked at the gun, making sure his finger was away from the trigger and that the safety was still on.

The General switched off the safety on his gun with a click.

Except for the rushing of the wind, the maglev train was silent as it pulled into the station, floating on waves of magnetism. The wind howled past their ears, as the train was moving very fast, before its quick deceleration and stop. Through the windows on the train, Leon could see people in the seats, both in uniforms and in regular clothing. The soldiers on the platform watched with interest and held their weapons at the ready.

The doors of the train opened and a soldier stepped onto the platform. He presented a laminated card to the senior guard, who quickly looked it over and scanned it with a laser reader into an electric device. Everything seemed to check out and the guard in command ordered his team to lower their weapons. Then, the passengers and crew of the train exited, under the watchful eyes of the security cameras, high above.

The General put his weapon away, and Leon followed along, holstering his gun.

"Come on, Leon. We're going for a ride."

"Where to?"

"Your new work site. We'll hop this 'lev here, but we're not going far."

The General lead him on board. It was spacious, with comfortable seats that had headrests and three-point seat belts. The General took a seat and started to strap himself in. Leon sat across from him and took a few moments to figure out the harness. The restraints in the elevator had been like car seat belts, but these were on another order of magnitude of complexity.

"These things go so fast, that you've got to strap yourself in like you're in a jet; we go that fast. Any suddenly deceleration and you'd be mincemeat."

"I bet," Leon said, and fumbled to get the harness on.

The train started to beep an alarm. A few of the soldiers came back on board and sat near the doors. They strapped themselves in and one of them entered a code on the keypad on the wall. The door closed gently and locked. Next, the cabin pressurized itself, and then the train started off, slowly at first, until they had cleared the station, driven by a pilot at the front.

Leon thought it was a strange sensation to ride on a train floating above the tracks, as the cabin shifted slightly from side to side, but it was mostly a smooth ride. The train sped up rapidly, and soon the wind was whistling by them, and everyone was held back firmly in their seats by the g-forces, making them weigh many times more than they usually did.

The lights in the tunnel moved by faster than any subway he had ever been in, blurring into nearly sold lines. He wondered how vast the maglev tunnels were that the secret military had constructed, and how wonderful it would be if this technology were able to be used by the public. It would revolutionize travel, he knew, being faster than any method of mass transit currently available. He watched the readout on the wall that clicked up towards seven hundred miles per hour. His body felt heavy and he had a hard time moving, as he was pushed back into his seat.

He saw a large doorway go past. It was almost completely blended in with the rock wall of the tunnel, but the light hit it in the correct way that it became visible.

"What was that door?" he asked the General.

"An entrance to another tunnel."

"Really? To where?"

"A private base."

"Private? You're kidding? Who could afford to build such a thing? And, why would it be branching off this secret, military tunnel?"

The General turned his head, heavy on the headrest, "There are a lot of very rich people in this world that like to prepare for any eventuality. And, a lot of companies who do the same. As for why they are sharing our tunnel, that's easy; it's a lot cheaper for them to pay us a lot of money to share the tunnel than to build their own and spend even more. Plus, the company that owns that base is a government company, anyway. But there are many other private bases around the world that have nothing to do with any secret D.U.M.B.s, and instead are completely independent. I'm surprised you've not run across them already in your career."

Leon fell silent, and spent the rest of the trip thinking and staring out the window. This was a whole new world he was being exposed to, one that had been right under his awareness for decades. And, for a man who made his living building tunnels, it was a blow to his ego that he had been left out of the loop of what was really going on in the world for so long.

Within a few minutes, the train started to gradually slow down, and finally came to a stop at another platform. The airlock seal hissed and the doors slid open. Leon, the General, and the soldiers stepped out to meet another group of soldiers. They saluted when they saw the General and let him pass right by with Leon.

The General led him out across the platform. It was still under construction and dirty. Workers in construction clothing passed by carrying equipment, cables, and pieces of wood; they were much like any construction workers, except for the guns they wore in holsters.

The General stopped and looked out over the site with him. "This station is being finished to service the new base that is under construction here. This is going to your first assignment."

"What's the main purpose of this base going to be?"

"You're going to get a full briefing on it, and meet your team as soon as we get to the temporary office they've got set up here."

The General took him from the platform to a small office that was built into a shipping container. It was outfitted with tight-fitting glass doors that kept out the wind from the tunnels and the ever-present dust. It's own AC unit with air filtration hung above the door.

Inside, he met the project manager, a middle-aged man named John Spencer, in military uniform. The General and John saluted each other, then the General introduced them both. After, the

General poured himself a coffee into a foam cup, made by the coffee maker they had set up on a small fridge. Leon couldn't get over how much the scene looked just like countless other construction projects he had worked on, minus the guards, uniforms, guns, and the technology he'd never seen before. He looked around for the donuts he knew had to be part of the scene, and was not disappointed when he pulled a double chocolate beauty from the grease-stained box.

John gave him some details on the crew and machines they would be working with, as the General sipped his coffee and read through his messages on his palm-sized, sleek, black, secret-project PDA/smart phone, the likes of which Leon had never seen before.

After the briefing, Leon was shown one of the weird PDAs by John, loaded up with the blueprints of the project, schedules, and build plans. The hand-held device was much faster than the best desktop computers he had used, and he was familiar with the best. The display was the clearest he had ever seen.

"The memory of these PDAs will be instantly erased if you take them from the base, and they will lock up, rendering them a useless hunk of plastic. They also have tracking devices in them, so they can be easily recovered. Do not remove yours from the base. They are for internal use, only," John warned, as he touched the screen, showing the various menus and applications.

"You've got your homework now," the General said.

"Yep. I'll be able to get up to speed with all of the info in there. Much more detailed than what was on that laptop."

"Go ahead and give him one, John," the General gestured to Leon.

John went to a cabinet, took out a new PDA and handed it to Leon.

The case of the PDA started to move in Leon's hand, seemingly alive.

"What the hell?" Leon shouted and dropped the device onto the table, as the General and John laughed.

"Gets them every time!" the General wheezed, doubling over.

"What was that?" Leon's eyes bugged out.

John got himself under control, though tears were in his eyes. "I'm sorry, I should have warned you, but the General likes to play this joke. The case will adjust to your hand, so that you can hold it very comfortably. Think of it as adjustable plastic that has memory. When you're finished with it, the case will expand back to its original dimensions."

"Memory-plastic?" Leon picked the PDA up again, carefully, and this time he was prepared for the device to start moving on its own. It adjusted to his hand, contouring to his grip as he held it, then slowly moved back to its original shape when he put it down. "That's amazing!"

"We do get some nice toys," the General agreed. "It's one of the benefits of being in these circles. There are quite a few other benefits, you'll see, Leon. The technology we use here on a daily basis is years, sometimes decades, more advanced than what you are used to in civilian life. I kind of take it for granted now. Take that PDA for instance; you can throw it against the wall as hard as you could and you wouldn't damage it. The batteries will last a couple of years without a recharge. Nothing short of a tank running over it will put a scratch on it. It has a memory of a couple of terabytes. It's totally waterproof, scratchproof, and dustproof. The case is impervious to EMPs, similar to the laptop you've been given to use. We've added the memory-material to this one, you've noticed."

He shook his head. "Incredible! And, that case is out of this world!"

"Out of this world is right," the General chuckled.

"I'm blown away."

"That's nothing compared to some of the other things we're using. You'll get to see them if you stick around for a while."

"This device would make an absolute killing in the consumer market! Apple would be done if this thing came out."

"Something like that will come out soon, but not until the time is right. Plus, I doubt most people would be able to afford it at its current state of development. And, we need to maintain our edge on technology. It helps us stay ahead of the game, and get things done faster, and better than anyone else; better than our enemies."

"How do you get the casing to react like it does?"

"I don't know. That's not my area. I just use the things. I can tell you that it came about as a direct result of back-engineering some of those downed UFOs. They have the most incredible things on board. The materials in those ships are far in advance of anything we've developed here on Earth. Some of those metals can only be made in space, and with minerals we don't even have on our planet. We discovered that their metals had elements in them that we didn't even know about. We had to expand our periodic table! What do you think of that?"

"This is getting more and more exciting!"

"I'm glad you're excited. There are a lot of reasons to work with us. Just wait and see. John, let's take him on a tour."

"Sure. We'll need these." John handed them each a yellow construction helmet with a light on it, and then led them out of the office and down the unfinished tunnel, past a checkpoint with armed soldiers on either side.

Soon beyond that, the concrete floor stopped and they stepped onto a dirt floor. The tunnel continued a couple of hundred feet further, ending with a large, white tunnel boring machine stopped at the far end, as big as a full-sized train engine, illuminated by work lights and being poured over by mechanics.

John explained, playing tour guide very well: "This is as far as the existing tunnel construction went, as you can see. We started excavation a few weeks ago and have made good progress."

Leon looked at the tunnel walls. They were circular, made of fused rocks and dirt that the tunnel boring machine had left behind, reinforced at certain points with concrete of a special design that seemed much stronger than conventional concrete. "It looks like you're doing quite well down here. I'm not sure what you need me for? Though, I'd like to learn your advanced techniques."

The General and John looked at each other, then at Leon.

The General spoke: "You have experience with some pretty large projects, Leon. Most notably the Chunnel, and that's one of the main reasons we wanted you on this project. Up ahead, the tunnel crew ran into an underground lake. It wasn't on any of our maps that were produced with ground-penetrating radar. The maps were only a few months old when we started construction here. So, you can see the problem?"

"Yes," Leon nodded. "A lake of any size doesn't just happen in a few weeks, without some dramatic cause. Were there any earthquakes down here before you started work?"

"No, none," John shifted on his feet.

"Then, how?"

The General broke in, "We found evidence of someone else's tunnel, newly built, running nearby to where ours was planned to go. It must have disrupted an aquifer. We investigated, of course, and it seems the Greys decided to expand without telling us."

"Do they usually tell you first?" Leon smiled.

"That was a figure of speech," the General turned around, looking at the tunnel, moving in the shadows cast by the work lights. "They don't communicate with us unless they want something. Most of the time they keep to themselves, and they most certainly *do not* tell us of their plans. And, we, of course, don't share our plans with them. In any case, this has left us in a bit of a bind, as their excavations diverted the underground water table in this area to the point that it flooded an underground cavern that we were planning to tunnel through and now it's an underground lake. What do you think, Leon? Is it going to be a problem for us to tunnel under it?"

He scratched his chin. "Without studying the survey maps and data I can't say with certainty. But judging by the geologic features of the area, I'd say it looks fairly solid. So, it shouldn't be an issue with diverting down under the lake, depending on the size and depth, of course. After I've looked at the data I can give you a better answer and a plan of action."

The General looked at John. "Very good. John, please give him anything he needs to make a detailed assessment of what we're up against here."

"Sure, of course," John nodded.

"I'll leave you here, Leon. I'm going back to base. Come on back when you two are done," said the General. He saluted John, then turned and walked back toward the maglev station.

Leon was given a full tour by John that went into great detail about the composition of the geologic layers, the water table, and the tunneling that had already been completed.

When they were done, Leon felt he better understood the problems at hand, and was able to give a preliminary recommendation.

"We ran into many unexpected detours on the Chunnel project and usually there was a good solution: dig deeper!" Leon told him.

Back at the makeshift office the two of them sat down to do some calculations and tweak the blueprints. By the time they were done it was almost dinnertime back at the base.

John took Leon to the maglev station and they rode to the surface, reported to the General, and then they all met for dinner to discuss their plans.

**

After dinner Leon made a call to Mary. She was taking it well, even though she missed him, terribly.

"When are you coming home?" she asked, on the other end of the phone.

"'I'm not sure yet. When they tell me I can leave. But I don't think it will be much longer." He gripped the phone tight as he answered her, knowing she was not liking what he was telling her. He sighed; if she couldn't handle him being away, he would have to throw in the towel and quit military contracting. The money was great though, and it really helped provide a nice nest egg for the family, and to save for Jennie's education.

"How's our little girl doing?"

"She's fine. She misses her daddy." Mary's voice was close to tears. "We both miss you."

"Me too, hon. Me too."

That night, alone in his room, he looked at the ceiling and wondered if it was all worth it. Then, his new military PDA buzzed as an email came in from John. He picked up the sleek gadget, and as it molded to his hand, a smile came over his face.
Cool!
Some things he could get used to.

6

"The new plans have been approved. You're ready to start digging," the General told Leon over breakfast.

Leon poured himself a glass of orange juice. "That's great!" He drank the juice quickly, as he was hungry, having stayed up late to tweak the plans and send them to John.

"Time to see how the rubber meets the road on this project. This is why we brought you out here," the General bit into a red apple.

"I appreciate that General. I think it's going to work out fine."

"I hope so. This project has already been mucked up once. We've got a lot more work to do underground, so the faster we can recover from this disaster and move on, the better."

After breakfast, they caught a maglev to the construction site. Leon met the rest of the dozen-men construction crew, as well as several guards, as John introduced him during an all-hands meeting. The civilian crews sometimes had women on them, but he noticed their conspicuous lack in this team. In his experience, Leon had found that a lot of women liked being down in tunnels. But this crew was all male, mostly made up of military recruits, specially trained in tunnel boring operations. They wore camouflage uniforms, with sidearms, just like his. They also wore military helmets with lights on them, like Leon also wore, but he found it a little strange; he was used to the usual white, or yellow plastic ones. A couple of guards with machine guns accompanied the group, and stood off to the side.

The crew were given the revised blueprints, and John told them that Leon was their boss for the tunnel boring part of the operation; direct orders from the General. Spirits were high as the crew now had a plan to tackle the problem they had run into.

Leon looked over the crew and at their weapons. They looked like a tough bunch, all fit, with crew cuts. He touched the gun at his side. He still felt strange strapping a gun on every morning, but since it was required, he couldn't complain much. Even though he'd seen, and touched, the alien body, he was still not convinced that aliens were a threat down below the surface. He just couldn't imagine how the Earth was inhabited by them.

I don't think there's anything to worry about; that body was from a crash-landed UFO, not from inside the Earth.

He smiled at the others and went around shaking their hands, "Hi, I'm Leon Verdat." He was still not comfortable with saluting.

That's right, try to convince yourself there's no danger down here, Leon. Just look at all the soldiers and guns to protect you.

Later that day, the new plan was put into action. Leon oversaw the huge boring machine as its angle was adjusted and sent on a lower trajectory, under the new water body. On his suggestion, a new type of drill bit was brought in that was more effective on the kind of rock they were drilling through. Changing a bit was no simple matter, as it weighed several tons and had to be moved out with a crane. But once the old bit was removed and the new one in place, the machine was tested and found to be working even better than before, thanks also to some performance tweaks that he had suggested.

He was eager to get to work, in order to quiet his mind, and decided to inspect the boring machine and give the team a refresher on it, in case any of them were unfamiliar with any of its workings. Plus, it would be a good chance to correct any issues he found, and replace any worn out, or damaged parts before they fired it up.

However, he noticed something strange about the machine: there was no exhaust hose. Usually, the big machines were powered by massive diesel engines, and the exhaust was carried to the surface by means of hoses fitted in series to the exhaust pipes. But there were no hoses attached to this machine. He got down close to the fuel tank opening and smelled no diesel fuel, either!

"Hey, John! I need to talk to you for a moment," he waved John aside, not wanting the crew to overhear.

"Sure, what's up?"

"What's powering this machine? It's not diesel. I don't know what to make of this!"

John smiled, "I knew you'd catch on before long, even with all of the excitement going on around here. No, it's got a new, pollution-free, energy drive."

"Energy drive? But how? What sort?"

John put his hand on Leon's shoulder, "Things around here are on a need to know basis..."

"And, I don't need to know? Is that it?"

"That is the case."

"You're kidding me? I'm supposed to help run this operation, and I can't even know what's powering the machine we're using?"

"That's right. But don't worry your pretty head about it; the machine functions normally in most respects. The only real differences are that you don't have exhaust and you don't need to refuel for years."

"Come on! You're all playing a joke on the new guy, huh? Ok, I get it. Very funny!"

John looked at him with a blank face, "It's no joke."

He needed a few moments to process this, then said: "Wow. Alright. I can't wait to give it try."

"Come on, I'll help you get it ready."

They walked back to the machine and climbed onboard, then started going through the "preflight" checks and fired it up. Leon never tired of seeing how the machines worked. Their large turbines moved slowly but steadily, with diamond drill bits to chew through the rock. With tremendous pressure and strength, the drillers moved through the Earth at the rate of several miles a day. A stream of water was sprayed over the blades, which were thirty feet in diameter, to kept the dust down. As the machine moved forward on its tank-like metal tracks, it spewed out a melted layer of crushed rock and dirt that coated the tunnel behind itself. Then, the new tunnel walls were sprayed with the special concrete mixture, making them much stronger than the solid rock had been.

The machine was running smoothly. Leon sat up top at the controls with John and a couple of other crew members, supervising the movement of the machine. A dozen other men were on the machine, too, adjusting valves and levers as it roared on. All was routine for a while, but then the machine broke though a layer of crust to reveal another tunnel.

Leon yelled for a halt to the machine, and John hit the big, red Emergency Stop button. The machine shuddered to a quick halt, forcing those riding on it to hold on due to the sudden jolt, or be thrown off.

"What the hell is that?" John asked. "It's not on any of our maps." He scrambled down from the machine for a better look.

Leon stepped down, too. The passage ahead was opened to reveal a tunnel larger than the one they were currently digging. This puzzled them, as it was obviously not one of theirs. Many of the crew took their guns out and held them at the ready. Leon climbed down the walkway over the top of the blades and peered into the tunnel. There were tracks laid down in it, not that much different than their own maglev tracks.

"What do you make of it?" he asked. "Some old tunnel, or something?"

John was silent for a long moment, then went stone-faced and straightened up. "Yeah. It happens sometimes. Other crews were down here before. They sometimes run into setbacks, or budget cuts!" He laughed, but his eyes looked scared. "Take five. I'm going to have to call this in and see what they want us to do."

Leon shut down the electronics of the boring machine. The crew got off and milled around, trying to get a look into the hole, but John and the guards kept everyone back. John spoke into his radio, and listened with a most serious expression on his face.

"Something's wrong?" one of the workers asked Leon.

"Yeah. Must have been another tunnel down here at some point. Funny how they didn't tell us about it."

"Maybe they lost the map. Government and all." The man shrugged.

"Must be," Leon smiled, but even he didn't really believe his own words.

John strode over to Leon and the crew, then spoke: "Ok, back it off. We've got another crew coming in to fill up the hole. Command said it needs to be done. Everything else is on need to know and you grunts don't need to know. So, move it back!"

The crew groaned, as backing up the massive machine was more work, and less fun than going forward. It took a lot more control, as any move to the side could bring the tunnel they had just dug down on top of them. But Leon fired up the massive piece of machinery, and they moved the machine backwards to the last junction, and waited there.

Soon, they watched a different crew move forward in a spraying truck. They fired a liquid where it was wanted, over the hole, sealing it right up. Leon walked forward and watched as the sprayer filled up the hole into the other tunnel with fast-hardening concrete. He had never seen anything like it before.

"What is that stuff?" he asked John.

"Our invention: super-fast hardening concrete. It starts to harden instantly, so you can build it upon itself right away, in layers. Really amazing stuff. "

"What I wouldn't give to have that topside!"

John grinned. "I'll bet. People say that about a lot of things down here. You'll get used to it."

He didn't know if he *would* ever get used to it; working and living in two worlds, with two vastly different levels of technology. Part of him was amazed by the things he was seeing and working with, but not having been aware of their existence before raised a lot of questions in his mind.

What am I gonna tell the folks back home? Nothing, I guess, at least not for a lot of years.

He watched as the concrete crew filled in the hole and spread the concrete around to make a solid seam.

Who made that tunnel, and why?

Surely, if it was a new tunnel of the Greys they would have told him. Or, maybe not. So many questions...

But then he was given the order to mount up and start the machine again, and they moved forward at another angle, away from the tunnel they had discovered, boring a new tunnel for hours and hours, until they were very tired and hungry.

Finally, the shift ended, and they were taken back up to the base. Leon looked at his watch and had a strange sensation to learn that many hours had passed since he'd gone underground, but with no light changes it was odd. It was something he had never gotten used to in all his years of working underground and always found it a bit disorienting.

After showers, dinner, and a time to relax, the General called an assembly of the tunnel crew in the briefing room. The order came over the loud speakers in the ceiling, which reached into every room on the base.

Leon entered the briefing room to see the General and John talking at the front of the room. He took a seat and watched the others file in, guessing this was a regular, daily event.

"Alright folks," the General called out. "This special debriefing is on account of what was discovered today; another tunnel. I'm not going to go into detail about that tunnel, it's purpose, or anything more about it. Suffice to say that there was an error on the map you were using today. You will not speak about this tunnel to anyone, even among yourselves. Officially, you had a regular day down there, you saw no other tunnel. There was no other tunnel. You didn't have this debriefing. This event never happened. Are we clear?"

People in the room nodded and several grunted out a "yes, sir."

"Good. Then have a good night. 0600 comes early. Dismissed."

Leon shuffled out with the group, puzzled. He noticed that the General and John stayed behind, watching everyone leave and talking together.

One of the other new workers was Frank Sanchez, who looked around Leon's age, and was a mechanic on the boring machine. He started the same day as Leon, and they had become friendly. They sat in Leon's room after the briefing, drinking coffee, and watching TV.

"What did you make of that?"

"What? The other tunnel?" Leon whispered.

Frank nodded.

"Were not supposed to talk about it," he said into Frank's ear.

Frank shrugged, and pointed to his ears, then to the walls and ceiling, indicating the room was likely bugged.

"Probably," Leon nodded.

"Ah, hell, everyone's talking about the tunnels, anyway, with all those conspiracy shows nowadays, Jessie Ventura and all that. Shit!"

"Still, we're not supposed to talk about it."

"Talk about what? Aliens? Secret laboratories making clones and stuff? Nazis getting ready to take over the world again?" Frank laughed. "I didn't see anything like that down there. What a bunch of crap!"

"Maybe you just haven't been to those parts, yet."

"Aw, come on! If that stuff was real there'd be no way to hide it with so many people involved; it'd be all over the news."

"Yeah, well...You've been in some places now that don't officially exist, so you tell me?" Leon fell silent, not wanting to jeopardize his position. He put his hands up in a "I don't know" gesture.

There's lots you don't know, Frank, but you'll have to see for yourself. I'm not gonna be the one to tell you.

Frank sighed. "What have we gotten ourselves into?"

"A lot of money if we play our cards right."

"I like how you think!" Frank laughed. "But at the same time, some of this is freaking me out. I'm thinking maybe I got in over my head here."

"Maybe we both did. But we're in for the ride now. Might as well enjoy it the best we can and such," he pointed to his lips, then around the room with his finger. He smiled.

"True. It is pretty cool in a lot of ways," Frank said, nodding, playing it up for anyone listening.

"You got that right!" Leon paused, remembering his family and home.

The air conditioning system hummed away in the uneasy silence, filling up the room with filtered air. Leon smelled a hint of ozone. "What are you going to do when you get home, first?"

"Oh, I think me and the girlfriend have got some catching up to do. Maybe buy a big, new bed with all of the bread I'm making here!" Frank winked.

"That sounds like a good idea," Leon smiled. His thoughts went to his wife, Mary. He flicked the remote control, looking for something to watch to take his mind off their situation, and settled on the "A-team."

"I used to watch this show!" Frank chuckled.

"Yeah, me too. It was hard to believe there were really people like that, but I guess now we know that there are."

"Yes. So much I watched on TV is coming true."

"Spooky isn't it? Of course, around here it's "Star Trek" and "Buck Rogers" time."

"You got that right!"

69

***

Leon had a hard time sleeping that night, which was no surprise to him, and spent some time laying in the dark, staring at the wall. The sounds of the base crept into his room: jeeps moving by his window, planes taking off and landing, people walking by and talking. It seemed the base never slept, and it didn't. There were 'round the clock activities going on, and shuttle buses arrived and left with workers every twelve hours. Some, like him, lived at the base for weeks, or even months at a time. He supposed it was necessary, as all the travel on a day-to-day basis, going back home every night, would be impossible, but it didn't make him like it.

He fell asleep a few times, but jerked awake with nightmares of being buried alive and trapped in tunnels. He'd not had those sort of dreams for years, since the start of his career. He usually liked it underground, so why he was fearing it in his dreams was most puzzling. He finally got a few hours of rest, but not nearly enough.

7

The next day in the tunnel, Leon noticed that the military guards they had with them seemed more tense than yesterday. They clutched their rifles more securely, and looked around a lot, jumping at any loud sounds.

Perhaps they know something we don't.

Leon supervised the tunneling machine throughout the morning. They plowed through the strata easily, making the new tunnel without incident. No more was said of the strange tunnel they found the day before.

On the lunch break, the tunneling machine was shut down, and everyone took a few minutes to eat their packed lunches, sitting in the dirt. Leon and Frank sat together, a bit apart from the others.

"Those guys sure are jumpy," Frank said, nodding at the guards. "What do you think's into them?"

Leon shrugged. "Maybe they were told more than we were. There must be something to it. Must have something to do with that other tunnel we found yesterday. Everyone's been on edge."

"I don't see how they couldn't know about that! Talk about infiltration! Someone's been down here before them, and I think we could all be in danger."

"I don't doubt that you're right, but what can we really do about it? If we try to leave they'll throw the book at us. I'd say we're in a good mess, now."

Frank finished his sandwich, not saying anything more. He nodded at Leon, and sighed.

The day wore on after lunch, and they crawled along on the machine, making the new tunnel, slowly, carefully, and ever watchful. There was something strange about the other tunnel they had found, but no answers were coming; at least not to Leon and his work gang. The General, however, knew different.

Above the tunnels, the General met with Base Commander Cohen in the conference room. They were the only two inside the secure, soundproof room, shielded in a Faraday cage to prevent any electronic eavesdropping, and the heavy door was locked. The large, pinkish, jagged scar on Cohen's cheek drew the General's eyes, but he tried not to look at it.

They were sitting at the conference table, looking at the screen at the front of the room, on which was a live, teleconferenced video feed of a group of twelve well-dressed, civilian business people gathered around an even larger conference table on their end.

An imposing bald man leaned forward and looked right into the camera, staring at the General and Cohen, "The Council doesn't care how much it costs; find out what these bugs are up to and make plans to stop them. We don't need any more delays." The man sat back and let his words sink in.

The General cleared his throat, "Yes, of course. Right away, sir." He nodded profusely, getting red in the face, and looked at Cohen.

"I will assist the General in any way I can, you have my word on that, sir," Cohen nodded too, and swallowed hard.

The bald man looked at the others around his table and they nodded at him. "We'll get back to you, soon. Good day, gentlemen." The man broke the connection, leaving a blank screen.

The General exhaled roughly, and wiped the sweat from his forehead. He got up and poured a big glass of cold water and downed it very fast.

"I don't believe this," Cohen sighed.

"Jesus, we dodged a bullet there, huh?"

"I don't need to tell you how much that...incident yesterday worries me. How did they get so close to our tunnel without our knowing it? This is a slap in the face, let me tell you!" Cohen was a career, secret military man, in his early sixties, and looking forward to a peaceful retirement in a couple of years. The last thing he needed was any drama at *his* base.

The General thought for a few moments, and then decided that since it was only the two of them, now, and because he had no other option, he told the truth, "I don't know. We've had the standard tracking systems in place, as well as advanced detection systems. There's even been some new systems in use here that haven't been deployed anywhere else, yet."

"And they still got through? And, so close? How is that?"

"If I knew we'd have them by now! You think I enjoy looking like a fool?"

Cohen slammed his hand on the table, rattling the coffee cups and saucers. "This is crazy! They're going to have my head on a platter for this," his shoulders slumped. "How dangerous do you think it is?"

The General shook his head, "They could have taken us out at any time, by surprise, if they were in the tunnel. But they weren't there. My guess is that they were planning an attack, but waiting until they had sufficient numbers assembled. I'd say we foiled their plans by breaking through to their tunnel sooner than they expected, thanks to our new civilian contractor, who's a tunnel expert. That's something positive you can put in your report."

"Hmm, perhaps, but you know there's going to be an investigation. And, we'll have to send a team into that tunnel to map it and see where it leads. We could be in for a hell of a confrontation if we meet any of them in there."

"Don't I know it."

"I'm not going to take any chances with this. Make sure that team has portable scanners and the latest ones. Any blood that is split is going on be on my hands. I need to watch this one closely; I'll be leading the team."

"You don't have to do that," the General said, "we've got more than enough experienced troops down there to..."

"Not with this type of threat, we don't!" Cohen yelled.

The General let this true piece of knowledge sink it. Few had faced the enemy down in the tunnels, but Cohen had done so, and barely survived. "I suppose that's wise. Not many have had the experiences you've had."

Cohen pointed to the scar on his face. "You're goddamn right they haven't."

Cohen left the General in the conference room and went down into the tunnels. He took a few well-armed soldiers with him on a maglev, and rode it to the end of the line, going to catch up with Leon and his crew. They carried boxes of new hand-held scanners.

When they reached the end of the maglev line and the construction base camp, they got into four-wheel drive Humvees that were also running off clean energy sources, so as not to produce fumes in the tunnels. They rode through the new tunnel, passing by the sealed up area that the boring machine crew had broken through to the day before, exposing the other tunnel.

Shortly, they caught up with Leon and his team on the tunnel boring machine. Leon slowly brought the huge machine to a halt and they all got off to meet Cohen behind the machine.

Cohen walked into the newly dug tunnel with a wary eye on the scanner in his hand. It detected heat from living things, and was set to key off the heat signatures of the Greys, who had a different body temperature than humans, and it could penetrate thick rock walls, with a range of several hundred feet. The scanner was a marvel of military black budgets and it was many times stronger than a similar FLIR device used by civilian fire departments and police to see heat sources, like human bodies, through building walls. If a Grey were within range, then depending on the settings of the device, the scanner would emit either a loud beeping, or a vibration in silent mode.

Cohen didn't tell them the scanners were to detect Greys; they would find that out soon enough, if it came to that. Instead, he merely said they were to detect underground temperature fluctuations. As he issued the scanners, he told them: "You're going to notice something strange with these devices. They contain some very advanced technology that..."

Frank screamed and dropped his scanner, his cry echoing in the dark reaches of the tunnel.

Cohen continued, "Very advanced technology that molds itself to the hand of whomever is using it. But don't be alarmed, it won't hurt you a bit." He patted Frank on the shoulder.

Frank was rubbing his hand, and looking it over in the light of his helmet.

"Go ahead, pick it up," Cohen pointed to Frank's scanner lying on the tunnel floor.

Frank, seeing that the others were getting on fine with their scanners, reluctantly picked his up, and winced as the material contoured to his hand. He put it away into a pouch on his belt, quickly, touching it as little as he could.

Leon grinned and clipped his scanner to his belt, so he could work the tunnel boring machine's controls.

Cohen thanked them all for their time, and saluted them as he turned to go. The crew got back to work, and Leon gave the signal to start up the machine. Soon, they were moving along at a good pace again, carving the new tunnel as they went.

***

Work went fine for several hours after that, the rhythmic movements and noises of the machine sent Leon into a light, pleasant reverie, and he thought of Mary and Jennie, so far above and away, and wondered what they were doing. He took glances at his scanner now and again, but it was reading all clear. Things were going so well that some of the crew were becoming bored, even a little sleepy, as riding on the machine did get to be a bit hypnotic if it went along for a long stretch without any incident.

But Leon was never bored, as there was always the odd geode or crystal to look out for, that was cast off by the machine. When a good-looking one passed by, he would quickly pull it out of the wall. Soon, he had a small pile of nice-looking stones at his feet, with the best ones in his pocket for his wife and daughter.

It was frightening the first time the scanners went off: a loud beeping came from the devices in multiple directions. Hands went to guns, and to silence the devices. Then, the workers and soldiers looked around for threats with their eyes wide. But no one saw anything behind them in the beams of the spotlights from the machine, beyond which was a blanket of darkness. The blips on the screen soon disappeared. John decided that it was a malfunction, and told Leon to keep the machine moving forward, cutting into the rock and dirt, making the new tunnel.

Then, the scanners screeched out their warnings a second time.

A call from Cohen came over the radio, and soon Cohen and his guards were behind the boring machine, again. Cohen called up to Leon, making a motion across his throat, "Cut it!"

Leon looked at John, "Let me do it this time!"

"Go ahead," John shrugged.

Leon hit the Emergency Stop button and the machine halted in seconds. He'd never seen anything like it, and watched the machine in wonder, momentarily forgetting about the alert that had caused the shutdown, he was so enraptured in the mechanics. No boring machine in civilian operation could shut down so quickly.

Must be nice to have unlimited budgets to design machines like this!

He silenced the alarm on his scanner and pulled his gun from its holster. His heart rate was way up, and he was breathing fast, and starting to sweat.

Why are these damn tunnels so hot?

"Folks, at ease! This is only an alarm test! I repeat, this is only a test! There is no immediate threat, so you can holster your weapons," Cohen called out.

"But those readings? Those alarms? Were not real?" John held his scanner up, shaking it.

"No, we generated those blips."

"You almost gave us all heart-attacks!" John said.

Leon felt his heart start to slow down, and breathed out a sigh. He put his gun away, following the lead of the others.

"We had to test these scanners, and thought we'd get your attention," Cohen grinned. "But don't relax too much: we need to be very vigilant down here, especially with the discovery of that unknown tunnel. Threats could be nearby at any time. You must always be on alert and able to react in an instant. Ok, let's get back to it." Cohen motioned to Leon, winding his finger in the air, the signal to start up the tunnel boring machine again.

Cohen climbed up to the observation deck of the machine, just above the cockpit. From there he could watch the solid rock in front as it was ground up and liquefied before his eyes. The soldiers that came with Cohen scrambled to follow him up before the machine took off.

"You're riding along, now?" John asked.

"Might as well. I want to see how this team operates. You've got a lot of new men here," Cohen answered.

"Fair enough," John agreed.

Leon wiped his sweaty brow and fired up the machine. It came online so quickly and smoothly, he could not get over it. He smiled to himself.

They got back to work and continued boring into the ground, deeper and deeper, pushing ahead to some unknown goal.

Frank leaned over to Leon and shouted into his ear, over the roar of the machine, "How long is this tunnel going to be? Have they told you?"

Leon shook his head, "Nope. Nothing. I'm as much in the dark as you are."

"Great!" Frank settled back in his seat near Leon, watching the glow of the LED gauges on the instrument panel.

Then, the great machine died and started to wind down. The spotlights faded and the tunnel went dark. The blades of the machine ground to a halt and they faced a dead end.

"What the hell?" cried Leon, and looked over to John, who shrugged.

The emergency lights of the tunnel machine came on, casting an eerie yellow glow over everything they touched.

Cohen jumped down to the cockpit. "What happened?" he looked nervous and was gripping his gun tightly.

"I don't know yet. The power just gave out unexpectedly. We've got to run a few checks, then I'll have a better idea," John answered, not looking at Cohen, but staring at the gauges with Frank and Leon.

"Yeah, ok," Cohen said. Then, he called into his mic and advised the surface of the situation.

"What do you think it is?" Frank was searching through menus on the screens, looking for an answer.

"I really don't know. There's nothing I can see," answered Leon, looking worried.

They checked all of the controls, but nothing was giving them any clues about why the machine suddenly halted.

Cohen peeked his head into the cockpit again. "Well, you guys? Anything? We can't have this thing stopped for too long, or there will be questions, you know that!"

"I know," nodded John. "But if we can't find anything wrong, what am I supposed to tell you? It just died and we don't know why...yet."

"What?" Cohen said, his eyebrows raising. The scar on his face looked strange in the yellow lights. "You mean, it just stopped? For nothing?"

"Looks that way," John shrugged.

"Shit!" Cohen tugged at his mic. "Control! We've got a situation down here. Our crawler is dead in the water for no reason. Over."

"What? What's going on?" Leon was standing now, looking at the crew on the floor of the tunnel, harshly illuminated in the emergency lights. They were pulling out their handguns, checking them over, making sure they were ready.

"Get the laser rifles out, now!" yelled Cohen and jumped out of the cockpit. He went to the backside of the machine, where one of the crew was fumbling with a hatch, and couldn't seem to get it open. "Stand aside!" ordered Cohen, then he thumbed the combination on the lock and sprung the hatch open. Inside the compartment were dozens of black, sleek-looking rifles. Cohen grabbed one and held it up. "Everyone get a rifle, right now! This could be it!" He handed one out to each man who filed past.

Frank watched the commotion below. "This could be it, what?"

Leon shrugged. "Guess there are some better guns they weren't telling us about."

"Fuckin' typical!"

Leon and Frank made their way out of the cockpit, down to the back of the machine where they grabbed a rifle each.

"These are laser rifles," Cohen explained. "Take off the safety here. Do it now!" he demonstrated for them all to see, on his rifle. "I'm very concerned that our machine just stopped with no apparent cause. This has happened before; the last time we were attacked down here. Be on your guard. I've radioed the surface, but it will take some time for them to reach us with a transport. We're going to start walking back. Follow me." Cohen turned and led them back towards the base, through the newly formed tunnel.

"Attacked by who?" Frank called out, but no answer came.

"Move it! Now!" John yelled, and jumped out of the cockpit, the last one out.

Leon and Frank fell in the back of the line, following Cohen. They walked at a fast pace, though most of them didn't know why, into the blackness of the tunnel they had just come through. Even though there were a few of them, their helmet lights seemed woefully inadequate at penetrating the gloom.

"What do you think this is all about?" Frank turned to Leon.

Leon didn't know how much he should say, or if the others knew what he did about the Greys, so he kept his mouth shut and just shrugged.

"Watch out for the tunnel trolls!" one of the men called out.

"And, the demons and ghosts!" answered another.

"Probably little green men, too!" someone laughed.

"Shut up, all of you!" Cohen hissed.

They all went quiet and kept moving, into the darkness, away from the emergency lights of the tunneling machine, back towards the base. Leon looked at Frank and could tell that he was afraid.

Cohen switched on a light on the top of his gun, and it helped to light up the tunnel in front of him. The rest of them found the switches on the tops of their rifles and turned on their lights, too. They marched ahead, following Cohen and his guards, not saying much more.

A bright, green light flashed ahead of Cohen, and a round hole, big enough for three men to stand abreast in appeared in the side of the tunnel ahead of them.

"Shit!" yelled Cohen. "It's them!" He started firing his laser rifle at the hole. Bolts of blue laser light shot out from his gun, extremely bright in the dark tunnel, temporarily blinding everyone, accompanied by a loud, high-pitched "FOOSH!" noise. The laser blasts melted the rock where they hit and ignited it into flames. They all were seeing afterimages from the laser blasts when they closed their eyes, like camera flashes made, but there was no time to recover. Green light was spilling out from the opening.

"Back! Back! Retreat!" Cohen was yelling, as he ran backwards, firing his laser rifle at the opening. "It's the Greys!"

For a moment most of the men were in shock and stood watching as small grey figures with thin arms and legs, large heads, and oval, black eyes started to crawl out of the opening: Grey aliens. When the Greys started firing their green laser beams (with their own high-pitched ZING! sound) on them, over and over again, it was enough to shake the men out of their shock – the ones who hadn't been cut down already.

Cohen got a few feet down the tunnel, pushing through the frozen men, back towards the stranded machine, when he was hit in the head by a green laser blast and his head exploded, coating the walls of the tunnel in his blood and brains.

The men started to fire back, but not being used to the weapons they didn't have very good aim. Most of them ran back towards the boring machine, trapping themselves in the tunnel.

"Holy, shit!" one of the crewman yelled, and started firing wildly as he ran backwards, past the others. Then he was hit with one of the Grey's lasers and cut in two.

The first men to reach the boring machine crouched down on either side, getting what cover they could and returning fire. They stared as the Greys advanced, shooting, with their blank faces, shiny black eyes, grey wrinkled skin, spider-like limbs, and bulbous heads, not believing they were real. But when the Greys kept firing on them, they started to have an easier time believing.

Leon and Frank had been at the front of the pack, but now that the group had turned around to retreat, they were closest to the aliens.

"It's aliens, I knew it!" Frank shouted, shooting behind him, shoving Leon ahead of him. "Goddam it!"

Leon kept running, his heart racing with fear. He ran down the dark tunnel towards the faint glow of the emergency lights of the machine they had left behind. He could hear screams and laser blasts from the others as they turned to fire back at the aliens coming for them.

This can't be real? Is it?

Even though he had been shown a dead Grey before, he still had a hard time believing they were really there. He knew that when the mind was confronted with concepts it was unfamiliar with, it sometimes refused to accept them. He could only imagine the confusion and fear the other men must be going through.

The tunnel flashed with green and blue light from the lasers, and started to fill with the smoke of burning flesh, both human and alien. The aliens stank on their own, worse than any rotting smell any of them had ever smelt, but when their flesh was seared by lasers, it was even more nasty.

Leon saw shots of green laser beams flying over his head from their pursuers and ducked. The crew had retreated to the dead end where the machine had stalled. They had no choice of direction once the tunnel had been compromised between them and the base – their only way back to the surface.

Between a rock and a hard place.

Leon slowed as he approached the tunnel machine, its emergency lights seeming very bright after the darkness of the tunnel. There was a stillness there and it was quieter, more removed from the battle going on down the tunnel, but not for long. There was nowhere to go, and he turned to watch the white lights on the guns and helmets of the men bobbing around as they ran towards him, screaming. Behind them, he could see blasts of green lasers cutting them down, their flesh burning and smoking where the energy beams tore into them, their blood spattering in the air before settling in the dirt.

"Oh, my God! What are we going to do?" Frank wiped away the sweat that was streaming down his face.

"Get into the cab. Maybe we can get it going. We'll get some cover, at least. Come on!" Leon scrambled up the stairs, missing some steps, but managing to pull his heavyset frame up. "You guys!" he called down to the crew hiding at the sides of the machine. "Get on board, and keep shooting back! I'm gonna get us out of here!"

Frank looked back at the carnage, then followed him up, turning to fire when he could. The other men reluctantly started to climb back onto the machine, making attempts to shoot back, but it was clear they were terrified, and not good shots with shaking hands.

Leon put his rifle down and busied himself with the controls, seeing if he could get the machine going again. Standing on the top, he watched in horror as he could see another doorway opening in the tunnel wall beside them. A round portion of the tunnel became outlined in green light, then it shimmered and disappeared, leaving another gaping hole.

A green laser blast shot out from the new hole, right at him. He ducked and instinctively raised his hand to shield himself. The beam blasted off the last two fingers of his left hand, instantly cauterizing the wound. The cut off, burning fingers fell to the ground, smoking, and bloody. He looked down at his hand, at first not believing what he was looking at. It happened so fast, there was no time to react. But then the pain began to set in, and he started to scream.

He screamed even louder when he saw the Grey alien come running forward out of the hole with a laser ray gun. It was a different weapon from their human-made laser rifles. Where their rifles shot only a bolt of laser energy, the guns of the Greys could also let out a steady beam that cut through everything it touched. The Grey's weapons were far more powerful than anything the humans had.

The first Grey out of the newest opening began shooting wildly, cutting several of the men wide open, and shearing limbs off others. Some of the crew managed to fire back at the Grey, but they were ineffective, as several other Greys rushed forward firing their own ray guns.

Leon fell onto the deck of the machine and pulled his handgun out. He realized they were trapped and surrounded. Without getting up, he tried to get off a shot at the Greys, but before he could, another blast hit him in the chest, giving him a serious wound and knocking him unconscious.

Frank was taking cover on the floor as well, and was on the radio calling the base for help. He managed to get a couple of bullets into a Grey who stuck its head around the blades and it died in a mess of its own black blood.

The crew were being massacred, as there were just too many Greys flooding through the holes in the tunnel to be stopped with the number of crew who could still fight back. The green laser blasts tore through the tunnel with a fury. It seemed like more Greys were climbing through the holes every minute.

A maglev arrived at the end of the line within minutes, carrying a group of about twenty soldiers with laser rifles, machine guns, grenades, and rocket launchers. They had faced trouble with the Greys in the tunnels before, though it was not widely known; the organization liked to keep it as quiet as they could. They crammed into a series of Humvees that were waiting at the construction site, piling their weapons on the roof carriers, and sped down the newly built tunnel to engage the Greys.

A couple of the Humvees stopped near the first hole the Greys had made, and the soldiers lept out, giving covering fire to the other Humvees that continued on to the tunnel boring machine. They quickly beat the Greys back with shoulder-mounted rockets, filling in the hole they had made.

The Humvees that continued stopped near the tunneling machine and the soldiers got right to work; some of them laid down covering fire as others dragged the wounded out. Once the wounded were pulled back to safety, the soldiers really got serious, firing grenades into the second hole. Greys flew through the air as the ordinance exploded, some smashing their bulbous heads open on the rocky ceiling and walls. A couple of the Greys caught the grenades and threw them back, causing a few soldiers and crew to be torn to pieces.

The soldiers opened up with the rocket launchers, hitting the ceiling near the Grey's second hole in the tunnel wall, causing it to fall in and fill up the tunnel, partially burying the boring machine. They made short work of any Greys left behind with bullets in their skulls, or frying them with lasers.

The wounded, including Leon, were put into Humvees and evacuated to the construction site, then aboard the maglev and whisked back to the base.

Leon floated in and out of consciousness. He hurt, and he had never seen so much blood and gore in his life. And, not just human blood and guts, but he had seen the insides of several aliens, too. He was in shock, shaking in the maglev car on the way back to the base. He winced in pain as one of the soldiers, a medic, held a bandage pack to his chest, trying to stop the bleeding.

"Tell my wife and daughter I love them...and that I'm sorry I had to go away," he gasped.

"You're gonna tell them yourself. Just hang on," the medic stuck an IV of plasma into his arm vein, then patted his shoulder and moved on to help another wounded man.

At the maglev station, Leon and the others were loaded into the elevator and they shot up to the surface going at full, gut-wrenching speed.

They were back at the base in minutes and a medical team was standing by with stretchers and wheelchairs to get the wounded into the medical wing. Leon was lifted onto a stretcher and pushed past the General, who was watching the wounded being unloaded.

"Take good care of this man!" the General shook his head. "You're gonna be ok, Leon. You hear me?"

Leon managed to groan out a sound before blackness overcame him. He was taken right into the operating room.

8

"How...bad...is...it?" Leon asked as he woke up from surgery. His eyes were fuzzy, and he hurt in his chest and hand. When he could open his eyes all the way, he saw a large bandage on his chest and hand, slightly leaking with blood, and tubes running out of both. There was an IV in his arm with blood going into him.

"You're lucky to be alive. Most don't survive a direct Grey laser blast hit like you did," the General sat in a chair by his bed, watching him. "I'm sorry this happened, Leon, but you're going to be fine."

"I guess it comes with the job, huh?" Leon's dry voice creaked.

"That it does. Now, get some rest. I'll give your wife a call and tell her your gonna pull through, ok?"

"Thank you," he answered, before dropping off into deep sleep, again.

***

It was a couple of days before Leon regained enough strength to go back to his own room on the base to recover further. He would be sent home soon, when he was a bit stronger to travel. He had spoken to Mary on the phone by then, and all he would tell her was that there had been an accident, and some of them had gotten hurt. He was pretty sure it was classified information, anything that happened underground, but he'd have to check with the General to be sure.

Still, he didn't think he was ready to start explaining to her about aliens in his weakened state. He might never be ready for that conversation with her, as the likelihood of her accepting the fact of an alien presence on Earth was very small.

His days following the surgery to seal up his chest and treat his hand were filled with painkillers and a foggy brain. At least they gave him enough pills that he didn't feel much. The General came by to see him every day, sometimes several times a day.

The General sat on the edge of Leon's bed and put down the lunch tray he'd brought from the kitchen. "The food's not bad today, but I'm sure it's better with some of those pills you're on!"

Leon smiled, but didn't want to laugh, as that hurt his chest.

"Listen, Leon. I'm sorry this happened to you. If I had known you were going to encounter those damn Greys, I would have warned you. But those bastards have a habit of surprising us, and when they do, they like to shoot first. We do the same when we come across them, as we've learned from hard experience that they most certainly are not our friends."

Leon had to chuckle, even though it hurt. He was thinking about stories of friendly aliens, but the truth was far from the fantasy. "They're not E.T., like in the movies, huh? It's not your fault. You told me about the risks, and I took them," he shrugged. "I knew what I was getting into."

"Still, whenever a civilian comes to work with us, I feel responsible. When something like this happens, well...it's tough all around."

"Don't beat yourself up. What's done is done. I'm going to survive."

The General fell silent for a moment, looking at the floor. "When you want to leave, we'll get you home, first class treatment. And, if you want to cancel your contract with us, we'll pay you out, with a generous extra amount to aid in your recovery, no questions asked."

"Let me get well first, then we can talk about what happens next."

The General nodded. "Fair enough. As soon as the doc says you're well enough to travel, I'll see to it personally that you get home as soon as possible."

"Thank you," he said, weakly.

The General stood up and patted him on the shoulder. "And, don't you worry; we'll get those Grey bastards! We'll fry every last one of them!"

9

A few days later, when Leon was stable enough to travel, the General drove him home in his personal limo. This time there was no drinking, but they did have cigars.

Leon had a glimpse of the aboveground world as they were getting into the limo, and it was good to be outside again. The wide open space made his soul sing and his heart flutter, but the heavy thoughts of the aliens had quickly pushed his mood back down, and his still-painful wounds brought his attention back to the simple tasks, like moving around. Now, he'd have to wait until he got back home to see the outside world again, as the limo windows went dark on both sides.

"Have you had a lot of run-ins like that?" Leon lay his head back on the seat, glad of its comfort and support. The unseen world outside slipped by, as they crept farther away from the base and closer to his home.

The General leaned in to him, to emphasize his words and he lowered his voice, "I'm not supposed to say much about those incidents, but yes, they seem to happen on a fairly regular basis, hence the standard issue sidearms."

"I was wondering about that. Not too many foreign armies, or agents down below to be on guard against, at least from what I knew about before."

"That's right, very true," the General puffed on his cigar. "It's been happening more frequently, now. I think the Greys have been making a big push to get more of their underground network established in recent years."

"But why?"

"It's a complex issue, Leon. We have good intelligence that strongly suggests we may need to retreat to the underground cities for a time in the not-so distant future, due to planetary calamities. I'm sure the Greys know this, too. Hell, for all I know they might even be the cause of it! I wouldn't put it past them, those stinky bastards." He chewed hard on his cigar, making it a pulpy mess.

"Due to the sun? Solar flares?" Leon stared at the TV, not making eye contact; he was nervous to ask what sort of threats, as he knew very well the reasons for constructing the underground cities and bases, and none of the scenarios were good. They consisted of various factors from the invasion of a foreign force, a pole shift and massive Earth changes making the surface uninhabitable, an EMP pulse, or a solar flare that took down the electricity grid (and society with it), to the ultimate disaster; a full scale nuclear exchange. Still, he wanted to hear the reasons from an "insider."

Though, I'm an insider now, too.

The thought chilled him.

"That's part of it. The weather on Earth *is* changing. There's no telling what disasters are going to occur, but there is the potential for great upheaval, on a global scale. The world leaders know all this. I think they should just come clean to the people and tell them, but that's not gonna happen. Though, it's getting pretty obvious things are shaking up. But I'm not the one in charge, I just follow orders." The General shifted in his seat, took out another cigar and lit it up. "Want one?" he offered the cigar box.

Leon took a cigar out, but didn't light it. He smelled it, running it under his nose. It smelled rich, and he put it in his shirt pocket for another time.

"So, the government – our government – has known about the Greys since at least the Roswell incident, in what, the 1940s?"

"Yep. Probably, well before that. Roswell was only the first public incident of its kind. There have been reports about UFO sightings in newspapers going back a hundred years or more. And, farther back than that you have cave paintings and aboriginal legends tens of thousands of years old; heck maybe older. Our history with ETs goes back a long way, only now it's become more intense for some reason."

"And, why do you think that is?" He looked at his bandaged hand, wishing that his government and the world had come clean a long time ago about the UFOs. Then maybe, he'd still have his fingers, as he'd not have gotten involved in tunneling for them, and the world would be a very different place.

"Things are changing. The world is connected now like never before with the Internet. We've got weapons of mass destruction, and we can travel amongst the stars, we..."

"What you do you mean "we can travel amongst the stars?" he butted in. "As far as I know, we've only been to the moon. Ok, further with robot probes, but not with people, right? Or, am I missing something? I have the feeling that I am."

"There has been a secret space program for decades. And, the moon landings are not quite what you thought they were. We've been all over outer space with our advanced technology, not known to the public."

He sighed, "I guess it's not a big stretch to believe that, seeing as how I didn't know much about what was going on under my feet."

"The Greys are not the only ones who can travel to other worlds, or who have highly advanced technology."

"So, where have humans been?"

"I can't go into that with you right now; you don't need to know."

"What? I've battled with Greys and you can't tell me about where our own people have been? Probably with my tax money!"

The General shrugged, "Sorry, Leon. It's above your security clearance level."

"Unbelievable!"

"I can tell you what you'll easily figure out, and that is that other countries have had their own secret space programs for a long time, too; it's like the wild west out there, let me tell you!"

"Anything else you *can* tell me?"

"Just some general things, stuff that has been talked about online for years: were getting into cloning. I'm guessing that other races have been taking more of an interest in us, as we've been growing up some as a species; if not in wisdom. Our threat level towards life on the planet and beyond has gone up, you could say. Unfortunately, we've attracted some of the wrong attention, like the Greys."

"Were are they from?"

The General puffed on his cigar. "That's what I'd like to know."

"You mean, you *don't* know?" He turned to the General, shaking his head. "How can that be? You've had contact with them for decades at least! Even had some captured!"

"Some questions are not easy to answer, Leon, even with huge budgets and black operations. The Greys claim to come from Zeta Reticuli, and that may well be true. We have tracked some of them there. Where they started from, who knows? They claim to possess the ability to travel trans-dimensionally, at least that's what the ones we captured told us before they died. That's probably true. And, perhaps most frighteningly of all, we know they can infiltrate our dreams."

"Good, God!"

"Yeah, it's a regular freak show, let me tell you!"

"How much defense do we have from them? I mean, if they can just attack us like they did?" Leon swallowed hard.

"They are pretty crafty. We have developed technology to keep track of them, and keep them at bay, but the problem is that *their* technologies keep advancing quicker than ours do. We suspect they are being aided by even more advanced aliens, and are trading *them* for advanced technology, just like the Greys have been trading with us."

The desert sun beat down on the limo, still hot even in the autumn, its beams glinting off the metal, its heat working the car's cooling system to the maximum.

The smoke from the General's cigar spooled around the backseat area, quickly getting sucked into the filtration system. Still, Leon felt a bit ill at the smoke, the heat, and the motion. He'd been used to being underground mostly, for the past couple of weeks, and in his weakened state he didn't have much stamina. With his good right hand, he gripped the leather handhold hanging from the roof for support, as the car bumped along.

"So, it's all true...the things I've heard? That Greys have been working with governments, doing deals, abducting people with the government's blessing, in exchange for advanced tech?"

"Sometimes, yeah. Sometimes they don't even keep their agreements, or give us anything – they just take who they want. And, we're usually not able to stop them."

Leon sighed. "What a world!"

"Oh, it gets more and more interesting the more you find out. The rabbit hole goes very deep my friend, very deep indeed."

They fell silent and Leon watched the latest custom created pop stars shaking their money makers on TV, while he puffed on his second, very delicious, Cuban cigar that he had finally broken down about and lit up.

***

This time, they stopped for lunch at a roadside diner, instead of driving right though. Leon was glad for the chance to get out and stretch his legs. He'd been in a hospital bed, then in his room at the base for almost a week.

After they'd ordered their food, and coffee was served, Leon stirred in some cream and his thoughts wandered back to the conversation they'd had in the limo.

"What exactly are they?" he asked in a low voice, looking around to make sure no one was listening.

"Who? The Greys?" the General asked.

"Yeah," Leon whispered.

The General saw his discomfort and smiled. "Relax. Not many people would believe the things we're saying, even if we could prove to them that it was the truth," he sipped his coffee and looked at Leon, right in the eyes. "Ok, I'll tell you more about them. I think I owe you that much."

"I'd say so!"

"When it comes to those critters, it's vague. Some of them we've caught have been physical beings, flesh and blood, like you and I, except their blood is black. They've had reasonable intelligence, but seemed to be controlled by a central commander, or program. Other ones have been more robotic, even having some non-organic parts, or metal, and so forth. Also, there have been some that moved in the more spiritual, or energy realms, and were like ghosts. Then, some move in human dreams, getting right into the mind. Very strange, to say the least. And, very hard to get a handle on. Are you beginning to see why some things are kept hidden?"

He nodded, pulling hard on his coffee. It was the best tasting coffee he'd had in a while. Though, what the General was telling him was freaking him out quite a bit, and he was drinking more coffee than he should have. He knew he'd be paying for it later, in the form of numerous trips to the bathroom, and perhaps a sleepless night; laying there in the dark, scaring himself with thoughts of aliens. "If governments were to reveal the UFO secrets, then we'd all know how powerless they really are against them."

"I think you're starting to catch on," the General winked.

The waitress served their food, refilled their coffees and moved off. When Leon was sure she was out of earshot, he continued: "What about some of the abductions being faked, to make the victims *think* it's Greys, when really it's not? What if it's government agents doing the abductions, and using hypnosis, or drugs, and disguises to make the victims think they are being abducted by Greys?"

The General smiled, "Now, you're getting into some weird stuff," he chuckled. "Could be. There are many secret groups out there, with many agendas. They don't talk to each other about their activities, and they don't talk to us. I don't doubt the possibility, at all."

Leon looked down at his plate and watched as his fork separated his pancakes. He had to eat one-handed, due to his injury, and the thought made him depressed. But he felt determined to learn how to use his injured hand to the fullest, and resolved to work on it as he made his recovery. He leaned forward and his chest hurt where he'd been cut by the Grey's beam, so he carefully put the fork into his mouth. He felt like his world was unraveling, like he pulled apart his breakfast with the fork. "This is all too much, I don't know how you can handle it. There must be lots more that you know. How do you keep yourself sane?" he shook his head.

"It's not easy. But the frequent trips to a nice beach help. You should try it. We get paid enough for that."

"Did we find Greys on the moon? I've heard that. Do they have a presence there? A base?" He looked around, his eyes darting as he asked the questions that were burning inside his brain. His curiosity was like a pile of dry wood that had just been covered with gasoline and lit by a match; leaping to life and hard to stop.

"Something like that. Now you are asking about things that are better left unsaid, at least at this time, and in this venue."

"Ah, ok. Well, I hope that we can pick up this conversation another time. I'd really like to know more."

The General looked at him, thinking back to when he was Leon's age, "I know you do. You remind me a lot of myself. I was very curious too when I first got into all of this business. When the time comes, and it's deemed you're to know more, you will be given access. But decisions like that don't come lightly. It might take some time. I'll hint again with this: a lot of the stories you hear are true. I'd say at least half of them. Some of the stories are just nut-cases spouting off, and some are disinformation designed to lead the curious off the track, but within those lay some truths. If you really want to know, you can verify some of the stories for yourself. That's my best advice for now. I can't say much more."

Leon looked at him and smiled. "Thank you, I appreciate it." He felt the General was being honest with him, and would tell him more if he could. As much as he wanted to keep asking questions he knew that he had to pace himself, and that some answers were going to take time – and maybe some questions would never be answered.

He felt a pulse of pain shoot through his injured hand, and thought of his pain pills. He searched through his jacket pockets with his good hand and felt a sense of relief just touching the bottle of pills. He took a couple and washed them down with a glass of water from the diner, wondering if it was full of fluoride, or some other secret additive.

Getting paranoid there, Leon...
I've got good reason to be, now!

After lunch they got back on the road and drove, seemingly endless miles. The pain pills had kicked in and Leon took a nap. The General looked him over, and kept smoking his cigars, watching the TV, as lie after lie rolled by. He laughed to see it all unfolding, "Stupid pigs, eating up all the slop they're served...if only they really knew what was going on..."

Hours later, the limo pulled into the parking lot of Leon's office. The General had offered to drive him home, but Leon insisted on retrieving his SUV. It would be a bit of a challenge to drive with his wounded hand, but he'd have to get used to it sooner or later. There was also a bit of pride at work, in that he wanted to be able to drive himself home, and for his wife to see that.

Wait 'till she sees both our cars in the driveway again, side by side...

"Well, here we are," the General said, as the driver opened the door for him.

"It's good to be back," Leon extracted himself from the limo, moving slowly.

The General hopped out and offered his hand to shake, "Hell of an adventure! Now you've got some stories to tell your grandkids about – but don't tell anyone I said that!" Leon shook his hand, and then they stood there giving each other awkward smiles. The driver took Leon's bag from the trunk.

"Get well soon, Leon. Let's talk again after you've taken some time off." The General looked him over, wondering if he would come back at all.

"Sure, General. Take care." He gave a salute. The General smiled and saluted back.

With that, the General got back into the limo. The driver shut the General's door, and then they quickly pulled away.

Leon didn't think he'd go back to work for the secret military again, but he wasn't sure. He *was* sure that Mary would want him to have no part of it, after he came home with his injuries. He was not looking forward to having to explain it all to her. She was likely to come unglued when she saw his hand, still bandaged up, and missing fingers. He thought it was better to call her first and warn her.

He looked through his bag for his cell phone. He finally found it and turned it on, then dialed his home number. Mary answered after a couple of rings. She knew he was on his way home, as he'd called her before he left the base.

"Hello?"

"It's me, honey," he smiled, trying to sound chipper.

"Hi! Where are you? Are you having trouble getting back?"

"No, no. Nothing like that. I'm at the office. I wanted to pick up my car and bring it home."

"Ah, that's good. Are you coming right home?"

"Yes, but there's something I have to tell you first."

"What is it? Is something wrong?" Her voice quivered on the line. She'd been worried about him for weeks straight.

"I want you to know that I'm ok, and I'll be home soon, but there is something that happened to me at the base, on the job. There was an accident. I got hurt a bit – but I'm fine. I didn't tell you this before, because I didn't want you to worry, not until I got home, and you saw I was alright. But I got my chest cut up a bit, and lost some fingers on my left hand, and I wanted to prepare you for that. And, Jennie."

"Oh, honey!"

"I'm ok, but it will take a little getting used to, and may look a bit funny at first. Especially with the bandages on. But those will be coming off soon. I also have a bandage on my chest where I'm gonna have a scar from a burn, but it shouldn't be too bad."

"Oh, Leon! I wish you'd never gone on that *damn* job..." She faded off into silence.

He listened to her breathing for a few seconds, then, "Can I pick you up anything on the way home?"

"No, just come home."

"I will. I love you. See you soon."

"I love you, too. Drive carefully."

"I will. Bye."

"Bye."

He clicked off the phone and decided to go buy her some flowers before he went home. And, a stuffed teddy bear for Jennie.

He got into his SUV and turned the key. It started right up, and he was sure to be extra careful driving. His wounded left hand would indeed take some getting used to.

I'd better be careful, it would be a damn shame to make it out of all that alive, only to get killed in a pileup on the way home!

As he pulled into his driveway, Mary rushed out of the house to meet him. She'd been waiting by the door. She took one look at his bandaged hand as he got out and her eyes filled with tears. She hugged him.

"Oh, my God, Leon. Oh, no, no!"

He held her tight and kissed her. "Come on, it's not as bad as all that. I'm here, now. It's ok."

She wiped her eyes and took a few deep breaths, calming down a little. He reached inside the car, pulled out the dozen roses he'd bought and gave them to her.

"Oh, they are beautiful! Thank you!"

"It's just a little token. I've got a lot more making up to do for you, and Jennie; I'm sorry that my work puts you through so much worry."

Jennie rushed out of the house. "Daddy! Daddy!" she yelled and grabbed his legs.

He picked her up, hugged and kissed her. "That's right, daddy's home now! I missed you, honey!"

She looked at his hand and touched the bandages. "What happened to your hand? Are you ok?"

"Yes, I'm ok. But I look a little funny now on the hand. Some of my fingers got taken off in an accident."

He hated having to lie to her and Mary about what the cause of his injury was, but due to his secrecy oath, he couldn't say anything. Even if he broke his oath and told them the truth, they probably wouldn't believe him. The thought that he had to keep something so important a secret from his family brought waves of stress over him.

Jennie saw he was upset and put her hand on his face, "Daddy! It's ok. I still love you."

That made him smile. He reached inside to the passenger seat and took out the teddy bear to give to her. She hugged it right away, then hugged Leon again. "Thank you, Daddy!"

"You're welcome." He put her down and tried to compose himself. "What about you two? How have you been? What's new?"

"I've been slow simmering your favorite all day, roast beef."

"Mmm! It so good to be home!"

"We're so glad you're home," Mary hugged him.

He put his arm around Mary and they walked towards the house.

"What should I call him?" Jennie asked, engrossed in her new teddy, trailing behind them.

"Whatever you want to," Leon told her.

"I'll have to think about it," she said. "It's a big decision."

Leon and Mary smiled at each other as they walked into the house.

***

Dinner that night was one of the most delicious meals that Leon thought he'd ever had, and he was surprised by how much he'd missed his family, and the small things they shared together that brought him such happiness. He'd been away from them before on business trips of the same duration or longer, but this one had been different from all the rest. He didn't think he'd ever been closer to being killed on a job, and construction work was dangerous at the best of times. For dessert Mary brought out a large carrot cake, also Leon's favorite.

"Come here," he said as she put the cake down. He gave her a big kiss and Jennie giggled. He always knew he had a good woman as a wife, but at that moment he knew how lucky he really was.

After dinner, as Mary cleaned up, he and Jennie lazed around the living room, watching Jennie's cartoons that she'd recorded on the Tivo. Usually, he watched Jennie's cartoons with her, so they had some catching up to do, as they had piled up.

Later that night, he read Jennie a story, and tucked her in bed. He stood by the door watching her sleep for a minute, before turning out the light. "Sleep tight," he whispered.

He made his way to the master bedroom, and then, after some initial hesitation on Mary's part that she would hurt Leon, and his assurance that he was feeling fine, they checked to make sure their sexual chemistry was still going strong.

10

Leon took a couple of days off to rest and regroup. And, to make up for the time he'd been away, he hired their trusted babysitter to watch Jennie, then Mary and Leon headed off for the afternoon.

They drove to a local quarry to do some geode hunting. It was what they did on their first date together. Leon knew the owner, and he let him hunt for rocks when the quarry was closed.

"Oh, this is romantic! Just like before we were married," Mary smiled and held his good hand.

He smiled back over to her, so very glad he was alive and that they could spend this good time together. It was about a half hour drive to the quarry, just north of the suburb they lived in. The sky was clear and blue, and the traffic was light, it being a Sunday. He pulled into the quarry and killed the engine.

The quiet surrounded them and surprised them, as it always did. The only sounds were of the wind and birds. The odd car passed by once in a while, shattering the calm before the sounds of nature took over again. Their feet crunched over the gravel as they walked. She flashed back to their first date, in this very quarry, over ten years ago.

He had first asked her out at a gem show. She had been working behind the table for a local bookstore that sold mostly spiritual-type books, but they also did a brisk trade with crystals and other stones. The store was where she had first met him, when he'd come in to browse the new arrivals of stones on a regular basis. They'd struck up a casual friendship, and she waved to him as he stepped through the crowd, up to her table. It was there that he asked her out on a date, and one of the things they did was go to the quarry to look for geodes.

She closed her eyes as the sun fell over her face, "Remember the first time we were here?"

"How could I forget. It was one of the best days of my life," he moved close and kissed her.

The younger Mary had been nervous to go on a date with the younger Leon. She didn't go on many dates back then, not because she wasn't good looking, or didn't want to date, but because she was interested in things that the average guys she met were not interested in, and found she had little to talk to them about. All that changed when she and Leon met. He knew more about rocks than she did, and it was clearly a passion of his. She never forgot how he amazed her on their first date by finding a large number of very nice stones amongst the clay and dirt of the quarry.

"Oh, my! How do you do it?" she had stared, her mouth open, as he pulled another nice geode out of the ground.

He shrugged and tried to appear modest, "I've always been good at finding them."

They had kept hunting until they had gotten hungry, and then found a spot to lay out the picnic blanket. Mary had packed a few sandwiches and root beers for them, and they made a picnic out of it, all alone in the quarry. It had been a warm summer day.

There was a vast open space in front of them, where the quarry had taken the land down quite deep. A hundred feet or so before them was a drop off, where the quarry walls went down sheer; a couple of hundred feet to a pond below, where rain had accumulated in the dug out pit. Birds flew around the water and soared on the thermals high above. They ate and looked out at the city in the distance, looking like a plaything, or a distant dream.

After, they moved closer and spent a long time laying together, kissing and exploring each other's touch for the first time.

She lay back, taking the hair from her eyes, "What does your last name mean? I've never seen it before. Does it mean anything?"

"I was told by my dad that it means courage."

"Very nice. It suits you."

He smiled, "Thanks."

"Was your dad right a lot? Mine always was!" she laughed.

"A lot of the time, yeah."

"Are you looking to be a dad someday, yourself?"

"Maybe? Do you want to make me one?"

They were so into their kissing session, that before they noticed it the sun had set and it was getting dark. She found herself taken with the handsome young Leon, but there was something else he wanted to show her, to impress her.

He jumped up and pulled her to her feet. As twilight glowed around them, he kept looking for geodes, taking her by the hand. He kept pulling the sparkling rocks out of the clay.

"How do you keep finding them in the dark?"

He smiled, even though she could barely see his face in the low light. "That's because I'm not using my eyes."

"But you're feeling for them? We just walked over to this spot, you bent down, and dug it out. And, you've done that several times now and it's practically dark. Did you bury them before, or something? You don't have to impress me, I already am," she laughed.

"Nope. I didn't plant them here. I've just been finding them now."

"Really? But how? If you can't even see them?"

He took his time to answer, wondering if he should tell her the personal thing about himself. But he reasoned that if he was going to have a future with her, and he wanted to, then he would have to let her know the real him. So, he took a deep breath and told her: "The crystals give off a frequency. That's why they use them in radios and watches. A frequency is another way of saying a sound. They give off sound and I can hear it. I guess my ears are just unusually sensitive." He'd not told anyone else about his unusual ability, and was unsure how she'd react. He wanted to prove to her that it was real before he explained it to her, so she would know he wasn't crazy.

"Leon, that's amazing!" she reached out to hug him. "I don't know if I could believe it unless you showed me, but you did!"

His smile was so big in the dark, the sides of his mouth hurt. He'd told her about one of his secrets and she was thrilled with it. He was a bit of an unusual person in a few ways, and he always was careful to hide it. But with her, he was starting to see that he didn't have to hide anymore.

They packed up and made their way back to his car of the time, a lovely old hunk of Detroit steel in the form of a 1967 Chevy Impala. He drove her home while he held her hand, and kissed her some more before dropping her off, parked outside her house with the engine off and the radio on.

Since that first date the quarry had been one of their favorite places to visit. Now, years later, they walked the quarry together again, reminiscing. He would stop every so often and pull a geode out of the clay to present to her. She was still fascinated every time he found one.

At the end of their visit they had several nice specimens to show Jennie, who was always thrilled when they brought home gemstones for their large collection. Proud parents that they were, they were happy to see their daughter was picking up their love for rocks and minerals, too. It was something else they could share as a family, which was very important, as Leon's work often kept him occupied, and his time with them suffered.

Watching Jennie examine the new rocks they brought her, he made a mental promise that he would spend more time with his family.

Before it's too late.

11

Leon couldn't stay away from the office long; it was his own business, after all. When he went back in everyone asked about his hand, of course. He chalked it up to a work-related accident and left it at that. Nancy had done a good job of taking care of things while he was gone, but there was a pile of paperwork that required his attention. He grabbed the heavy pile of paper and settled in to get caught up with it, and all of the emails, and phone calls he'd missed.

He sighed as he spun around in his office chair to turn on the computer. Getting caught up after a trip was always a pain in the ass. But now he had less fingers to do it with. He found it wasn't so bad though, as he was already getting used to just using the fingers he had left, and he was never much of a typist, anyhow.

Lunch time came and he decided to go out. He wanted to feel the warmth of the sun and see the open sky after being underground so much lately. It was usually like that for him; he had fun working underground, but he was always glad to get back up on the surface again. He drove to a nearby burger joint and had a big, greasy lunch, which upset his stomach some, but it sure tasted good going down.

When he got back from lunch Nancy told him there was someone waiting to see him. He looked around the lobby, but there was no one there.

"I asked him to wait out here, but he said he'd wait in your office, and he just went right in," she shrugged. "Sorry."

"That's ok. It's not your fault. Some people sure are rude, huh?" His forced a smile for her, but his chest was already getting tight, and making his still-tender wounds hurt, as he knew who was waiting for him. He walked into his office and sure enough, it was Mr. Black.

"Hi, Leon. Nice to see you, again," the strange man dressed all in black smiled.

Leon didn't say anything at first, he was too shocked; he just closed the door and sat down behind his desk. "Do you always have to make such a dramatic entrance? People are going to start talking. It's not right for you to just barge into someone's office like this.".

Mr. Black laughed and spread his arms out. "What are they gonna do about it? Do I look worried?"

Leon wrung his hands together on top of his desk.

The man looked at Leon's hands, "Got yourself banged up a bit there, huh?"

"You didn't say I was going to run into...*them* down there! I could have been killed!"

"Would you have believed me if I had told you? Your job is dangerous anyway. You'd still have gone, just to see if "they" were for real."

"Maybe, but it's still too dangerous. What if I had been killed? What about my family?"

"Many of those who work on our projects have families. They know the risks, and they still do it. You know the risks about your job and you still do it."

"It's not the same."

The man smiled and took out an antique cigarette case, then carefully withdrew a cigarette with his long, pale fingers, and lit it up. He blew smoke at Leon. "Don't be coy with me. You couldn't help yourself to go down there and you know it."

Leon stood up and opened up a window. "I didn't have much of a choice."

"Sure you did. And, you made the right one."

He sighed. "So, what are you doing here? I'm not ready to go back, yet. I don't know if I will ever be."

"That's fine, Leon. We want to you rest up and think about things. You did a good job down there. We owe you our thanks. We regret what happened to you and want to make sure you are compensated." Mr. Black pulled a thick envelope out of his jacket pocket and slipped it across the desk.

"A bribe? To keep quiet?"

"Your payment, and a bonus. It was in the contract."

"It's all here? In cash?"

"Believe me, it's better this way. There won't be a paper trail. That's protection for everyone."

Leon took the envelope the looked inside. It was filled with thousand-dollar bills, in US dollars.

"What am I supposed to do with these?"

"Put them in your bank. I'm sure they'll be happy to accept them." Mr. Black grinned and puffed on his cigarette.

"It's a lot of money, but I wonder if it was worth it." He cradled his left hand, as it was starting to ache. "I'm thinking not."

The strange man let the smoke out of his mouth in rings. "Sometimes knowledge comes at a high price. Just be glad you are still around to appreciate what you've learned and seen. Most people in this world will never get the chance to find out if certain things, or creatures, are real, or fantasy, like you have."

Leon sat back in his chair. "I'm not sure I believe it all happened."

"I can make you forget it, if you'd prefer? We have our methods that are quite effective. Just wipe out that section of your memory, and viola!" He darted the cigarette around in the air, punctuating his words.

"N-no, that's ok!"

"You see, some things in this world are just a bit of a mystery. That's how it is. The best we can do is to try and keep a handle on it. I don't pretend to understand it all, either. I don't know if anyone does. But us who work on the inside, it's our duty to keep the public protected from things that they just couldn't deal with. We keep the world running smoothly, just look at it like that."

"By keeping secrets and lying to people? I thought this country was free!" Leon was starting to get red in the face.

"Keep your shorts on; relax. We can't go telling people that little grey men are visiting us, and are living underground. That they have superior technology to ours. We'd lose our grip on the population; people would lose faith in government. We'd also lose our place as the top dog as far as other nations are concerned. It's not something we can readily admit, you must see that? I hope you do, so you'll keep your mouth shut. But if you don't...well, I'm sure you have an idea what the consequences will be?"

He pondered the questions, turning over the possibilities in his mind. "I don't know. I don't like the government keeping something so important to humanity a secret. There must be a way to let people know the truth?"

"Don't worry. The time will come, quite soon, when the secret will get out. Most people believe in UFOs and aliens, anyway. There will be no hiding it after certain events take place in the near future."

"Like what?"

Mr. Black stubbed out his cigarette on the floor. "That's all I can tell you for now. But stick around. Go back on assignment when the General calls you, and you'll find out more." He got up and extended his hand. "Good to see you, Leon. Talk to you later." They shook hands and then he left the room.

Leon followed him out and watched him leave through the front door.

"Who was that?" Nancy asked. "Looks like he's out of a movie, or something with those old clothes. Is he an actor?"

He nodded, "Yeah, some of our clients can be a bit eccentric. We do build bomb shelters, so it's to be expected." He chuckled, trying to make light of things, but even to himself, his laugh sounded hollow and fake.

He walked back into his office and locked the door. He looked at the envelope of money on his desk, then picked it up and put it in his pocket. Mary would be happy to see the cash. There was a lot they could do with the extra money; make some house repairs, and put aside something extra for Jennie's future. And, he did have to admit to himself that it was nice to have more money, but he'd have to do some serious thinking about going back underground with the General again. "What am I getting myself into?" he shook his head back and forth, and looked at his wounded hand.

12

Life returned pretty much to usual for Leon over the next few weeks. He spent time with his family and did some work on the house. They even took a vacation and went to Disney World.

But he could not totally relax, as he always had the thought in the back of his mind that Mr. Black and the General would call on him again. He was not sure what he'd do when they did. He kept the cell phone the General had given him off and away in a drawer.

A few weeks later they did call on him again; the General showed up at Leon's office. Leon was behind his desk, working on some calculations, when his intercom went off on his phone with a disruptive buzzing that broke his concentration.

I've got to change that phone!

"What is it?" he sighed.

"Someone's here to see you," Nancy's voice said over the speaker.

"Send them in."

He was not expecting anyone and hoped it was not Mr. Black, again.

The General popped his head in the door. "I didn't want to show up like this, but you're not answering your phone, Leon, and I thought this better than showing up at your home." The General raised his eyebrows and took a puff of his cigar.

Leon looked up from his desk. "Come on in."

He stood and met him in the middle of the room and they shook hands. The General was in a navy blue suit, with no military markings of any kind; the only things that gave him away were his crew cut, fit physique, and boots.

"Good to see you, Leon! You're looking good."

"Thanks. You as well. I assume you've come to try and tempt me back to work with you?"

The General grinned, "How'd you guess this wasn't a social call?" He closed the door gently and sat down. "Got a new mission for you. How are you feeling? Are you up for it?"

"I dunno. What is it? And, what does it pay?"

The General laughed and slapped his leg. "That's the spirit! Well, they got that tunnel finished, finally – the one you worked on. Went in there with a tactical unit and checked out what those stinking Greys were up to. It seems we drilled into one of their transport tunnels. They've got their own maglev system, can you believe it! I wonder if we got ours from them, or vice-versa," he puffed on his cigar. "You want one of these?" he waved the cigar in the air.

"No, thanks, I'm good."

"The Greys had come back after the attack you were in, and destroyed their maglev tracks up to the point we discovered them, melted them down to slag. Then, they buried the entrance we had made, and also their own tunnel for miles. We still haven't reached the end of it. But there's a section of their tunnel that remains, beyond the point where your machine was stalled. It looks like they have some structures in there that we need to check out."

"You're going after them?"

"Of course! We've got to teach those bastards a lesson!"

Leon shook his head and exhaled, "This is getting weirder and weirder. What do you need me for? It sounds like what you are doing is out of my area of expertise. It sounds like a military operation now."

"Not quite. It's mainly a tunneling operation, until we get through the mess they left and open up their tunnel as far back as we can. We could use your help. What do you say?"

"I don't think I'm interested. I've got my family to think about," he held up his wounded hand with the missing fingers.

"It would be worth a lot of money for you to come back down there. It pays even more than last time, naturally," the General put his hands behind his head and grinned.

"It would have to. I can't just take that sort of risk again for nothing."

"You'll get double what you got before. How's that sound?"

"That's a start."

"I'm sure you wouldn't mind getting revenge on those bastards that shot you, am I right?"

He thought for a few moments, and had to admit that the General was right. "Could be."

"Don't worry, we'll find them. And, when we do, I'll make sure you get a clear shot. We won't stop until we stamp them all out. How's that?"

Leon felt the lure of money, adventure, and now revenge, pulling at him. It was like a rope curling around his ankle and drawing him back, down deeper underground, into the blackness, into the dirt. "How long would you need me for?"

"Not sure. A week, or two. Depends how long it takes to dig through their tunnel."

"Do I have some time to think about it? Ask the wife?"

"I'll need your answer tomorrow, Leon. We need to keep moving on this."

"Ok, I'll let you know tomorrow."

"Good."

The General stood and they shook hands.

Leon walked him to the main doors. As the General left, he poked Leon lightly in the ribs, "And, turn on that phone!"

Leon laughed and rubbed the sore spot, then turned back inside as the General was getting into his limo.

"Who was *that*? Nancy looked out the window, watching the limo pull away.

"Forget it, he's married."

He went back to his office, closed the door and sat down heavily behind his desk. He looked at his maimed hand, then at the framed picture of Mary and Jennie sitting on his desk.

"Goddammit!" He pounded his good fist on the desk, shaking the pictures and the computer monitor. He got up, grabbed his jacket, shut off the light, and pulled the door closed.

"I'm going home early today," he called to Nancy, on his way out the front door.

"Are you ok?"

"Yeah. I'll see you tomorrow..."

Back at home, he dug out the cell phone the General had given him and turned it on. It still held a charge, but he plugged in the adapter to the wall for good measure.

The next night, after Mary and Jennie were asleep, he took the cell phone and went to sit in the kitchen and look at the moonlight in the garden, and drink some Scotch on the rocks.

The phone rang. He answered it quickly, afraid of it waking anyone up in the house.

"Hello?" he said with a husky, sleepy voice.

"It me, Leon," the General's voice said.

"I know."

"What have you decided?"

He swallowed hard. "Ok. Let's do it." He felt like a robot, playing out a written script, saying what he was supposed to be saying. It didn't even feel like him.

"That's my man! I'll send a car to pick you up in the morning, at 0800 from your office. Sound good?"

"Yes, that's fine."

"Very good. Have a good night."

"Goodnight."

Mary was icy cool when Leon crawled back into bed, woke her up and told her he was leaving on another secret government job.

"Are you going to come home in a box this time?" she said.

He stared at the floor for a few long moments, then shifted over to hug her where they sat on the bed. "Honey, I know it's hard to understand why I would do something like this again. I've been asking myself why I'm doing this as well, but..."

"Then, why, Leon? Do you want to leave your daughter without her father? Do you want to make me a widow?" she shook her head, nearly crying.

"It's something I have to do. I feel it's my duty. There are things about it you don't understand, and I can't tell you." He got up and started packing. "I'm sorry."

She watched him pack as she dabbed the tears from her eyes with a tissue.

For what was left of that night neither of them slept, and they stayed on their own sides of the bed.

13

Leon awoke early and had breakfast with his wife and daughter. It was a strained meal. Jennie kept asking him why he had to leave again, and Mary just kept quiet. He didn't eat much; no one did. When he was done he said goodbye to them mechanically and picked up his bag. Jennie didn't want to let go of his legs, and held on, sobbing. Finally, Mary had to pry her off him.

Mary gave him a hug and a small kiss. "Come home safe," was all she said.

"I will," he tried to smile.

The drive to his office felt like one of the longest drives he had ever taken. He started to tear up as he drove, and then it all really sank in: he was going back underground with the secret military.

But there are aliens there! Real aliens!

The boy in him still couldn't get over the fact that aliens were real, even though they'd almost killed him.

He was glad that he arrived before his ride did. He got out of his SUV with his bag and locked the car up. Then, he stood there, staring up at the faint moon still visible in the daylight, thinking about how humanity was truly not alone. "Amazing."

His eyes snapped back down as the General's limo pulled up. He had a sense of deja vu as the window rolled down and the General's smiling face greeted him again.

"Ready to roll?" the General winked, his cigar burning away.

"I am. Let's do this," he handed his bag to the driver and got in backseat beside the General.

They rode in silence for a few minutes, as the weight and gravity of the situation sank in.

"Did your wife give you a hard time about going back?" the General puffed away. He didn't seem too troubled, as for him this was routine work.

"She did. But what was worse was the reaction my daughter had. I don't think I've ever seen her so sad."

"Sorry to hear that."

He didn't think the General really did understand; he wouldn't unless he had family of his own.

"Are you married, General? Have kids?"

The General shook his head with the cigar still in his mouth. "Me? Nope, thank God! I was married once, but that was a long time ago. I'm an eligible bachelor, now!" He grinned, but his eyes were not smiling.

Leon looked over his face, knowing that the General didn't know what it was like to have to tell your family you were going away again, and might never come back. Twice. He looked at the grey hair on the General's head, and in his beard, and felt sorry for him that he was aging and didn't have a real home life, yet. Then, the General made the windows dark again, and they headed out on the highway.

They didn't talk much that trip. Leon had too much on his mind, and the General didn't really understand. They watched TV, with the General pointing out which news stories were real and which were fake, and having a good laugh over it all; they were mostly fake. Then, they both caught some sleep as the car swept through the hidden landscape, as day turned to night.

Hours later, they arrived back at the same base and checked in with security. It all went uneventfully, and Leon was given his old room back; it gave him a funny feeling.

"Home, sweet home, eh?" the General said, sticking his head into the doorway of the small room as Leon unpacked.

"I guess so, for now. I just hope I'm going back to my real home from this."

"Oh, you will. You're a tough old dog! I have faith in you," the General waved at him and left, trailing cigar smoke.

I hope you're not making a big mistake, Leon...

Sleeping that night was tough for him. He called Mary and let her know he had arrived alright, but it did little to reassure her. She wouldn't relax until he was back home and in her arms again. He tossed and turned, and got little sleep.

In the early hours of the morning, he lay awake and looking out the window at the moon. It was rising in a crescent, growing more full. "A bad moon, rising?" he said, then shut up. He didn't want to talk out loud to himself too much, as it would seem bad to anyone who overheard him; he was sure the room was bugged. Everything about being back there was straining his nerves, but he was committed now, so he resigned himself to ride it out.

But this is going to be the last time; after this I'm through with this stuff! That sounds like famous last words...

He breathed deeply and tired to calm down.

Finally, exhausted, he fell into a fitful sleep.

14

Leon awoke to the smell of bacon and eggs cooking. For a moment he thought he was back home again. There came a thumping on his door. He thought it was his daughter, Jennie. But it was Cathy, one of the base helpers, knocking on his door, trying to wake him up.

Shit!

He was running late, having forgotten to set his alarm. He groaned and managed to roll out of bed. He got dressed quickly in a new uniform that had been hanging in the closet for him. There was also his handgun and holster, and he didn't forget to wear them this time. His boots were there, and he slipped them on. They felt good, as they were broken in.

Just like old times.

He made a mental note to shine them when he got some time.

After breakfast (at least they fed you well, Leon had noticed), the General introduced him to the new work crew that had been brought in. The surviving workers who had been attacked with Leon were mostly too spooked to return, so had to be replaced.

Sounds like they were smarter than me to not come back!

The General led him into the hanger where the new crew was assembled, tweaking a drilling rig, getting it ready to go underground.

Jim, the head mechanic of the hanger was there, and greeted Leon again, with hand outstretched. "Hey, Leon, good to see you back." They shook.

"Howdy, Jim. How's things?"

"Oh, about the same. Busy, as usual," Jim tried to sound happy, but Leon detected an undercurrent of stress about him. Of course, with the General standing right next to them, Leon couldn't ask what was really on his mind, about the current state of the Greys, and if it was a wise decision to be going back underground at that time.

The General piped up, "Leon's ready for action. I trust you'll have the crew and gear ready this afternoon for the descent, Jim?"

"I will," Jim nodded. "Yes, sir." He gave a salute and the General returned it.

"Excellent. Carry on." The General clapped his hand on Leon's back to encourage him on; they walked. "Jim's the best mechanic and hanger supervisor we've ever had. I don't know what we'd do without him," the General chomped on his cigar.

"I can see why you like him up here, all safe, less risk of losing him."

The General stopped cold and spun to look at Leon straight in the eye. "Not losing your nerve, are you?"

He flexed his maimed hand. He felt it starting to hurt, or maybe he was imaging it. He wasn't sure. He was tired. "No, of course not, I..."

"Come on over here. I've got something for you," the General took him over to the supply room. "This time we've got some new toys to fend off those Grey bastards!" He held open the door and Leon walked in.

There was a soldier behind the counter, with a gun strapped to his leg. Behind him were rows of machine guns, ammunition, and other exotic weapons that Leon had never seen before.

"Hiya, General! What'll it be?" the man behind the counter saluted.

The General saluted back. "At ease, Jerry. This is Leon. He's a very special civilian who is contracting with us on some underground work. He's back for his second tour with us, and he's going to need some good firepower. He and his crew ran into some stinkers last time, and it wasn't pretty. We want to be prepared for anything this time out, and I think you've got just the thing."

The soldier nodded. "Indeed, I do. This is just in, and you've no doubt heard about it, General." He lifted an olive drab flight case onto the counter, about two feet long. Opening its padded lid, he produced a rifle with a futuristic-looking scope and oddly shaped barrel.

"A machine gun?" asked Leon.

"Oh, no!" Jerry explained. "This is a pulse-laser rifle! Brand new! The Remi EPR1." He handed it over to the General.

"I was hoping these would be in," the General raised the rifle up and sighted it at the wall. "How many have you got?"

"Two dozen; enough for your whole crew. You folks are going to be the pilot project for this rifle."

"Great," Leon sighed. "Hopefully they work when we need them to."

"Oh, they've all been given the green stamp. If they hadn't been approved, they wouldn't be here. You will be the first group to be issued them. But fear not, they have been extensively tested for reliability, durability, and effectiveness."

The General nodded and handed the gun to Leon. "These boys know what they're doing. If they say this weapon is ready to be deployed, then you can take that to the bank."

Jerry smiled. "Would you like a couple of them to take to the firing range?"

"Yes. In fact, call the whole crew in here and get them kitted up. We'll all go onto the range before we ship out this afternoon."

"Very good, General." Jerry picked up another case and put it on the counter. He opened it up. "The Remi EPR1 is the first of its kind developed by us. It's powered by a virtually inexhaustible power plant that works by extracting energy from molecular events on the subatomic level. It stores that energy, which is constantly renewing itself. We back-engineered it from a ray gun that was captured from the Greys. It was very complex, and took us a long time to figure out the details of the energy generation, replacement, and extraction cycle. But now that we've done that, we have a weapon that is capable of firing a variety of laser beams of various intensities, and that never goes empty. There are no cartridges to refill, or reload. The power supply should last forever; in fact, we've not been able to exhaust one of these rifles yet, even after millions of bursts. The barrel will melt long before the power plant shows any signs of quitting, and it won't even get warm until you've fired thousands of bursts continuously. It can shoot through plate steel armor, and will give those little Grey buggers a run for their money, even if they use force shields," he grinned.

"Force shields?" asked Leon.

"You haven't encountered that yet," the General cut in. "Some of the Greys have a device that encases them in an energy force shield. It's quite strong, and can turn away most calibers of bullets. I don't think it's going to be a match for this gun, though. We don't yet have one of their shields to test, but this thing has punched through any energy shields we've rigged up. Hopefully we'll capture one of those bastards with an energy shield so we can see what makes them work. They won't have the advantage over us for long."

Leon was given new body armor and communications equipment, including a helmet with a stronger light, and an ultra low frequency radio built in.

"Wow, I feel prepared now! Where was all this gear that last time I was down there?"

"We didn't think you'd need it last time. Our intelligence told us that the nearest Grey tunnel was hundreds of miles away. The Greys must have advanced their tunneling methods, or else figured out how to cloak their activities from us more effectively to get so close to our operations. We never imaged that you'd find yourself in a firefight. But now, the risks are greater, so we've upped our preparations and it's standard procedure now to outfit everyone who goes underground for combat, whether it's expected or not. Try it on for fit, go ahead."

Leon put on some of the new kit and took a look at himself in the full-length mirror. He still couldn't get used to seeing himself in the battle gear. He had on a flak jacket, flak pads on his arms and legs, gloves, and a Kevlar helmet. On his hip was the handgun that fired regular bullets. "Why the two types of guns?"

"Just in case," the General said. "We don't know if the Greys can block, or defeat the laser rifles yet, so we're not taking any chances. You'll all still carry conventional weapons as a precaution."

Jerry ran through the details of operating the pulse rifles, then the General got into his battle gear. Feeling, and looking like they were ready for action, Leon and the General made their way back to the crew. They received some hoots and hollers as they strode across the hanger.

"Nice gear! Looking sharp, sir!" Jim saluted the General.

"You're next! Get to the armory and get yourself kitted out. Then, send the rest of the crew over. We'll get briefed, then hit the target range afterward and get some time in with the new guns. We ship out tomorrow."

Jim swallowed hard. "You want me to go with you this time?"

"That's right, Jim. We'll need all hands on deck. I know you're not a fan of the tunnels, and I don't blame you. But you are the best mechanic I've got on this operation, and I need you down there in case things get tight. We can't afford a screw up like last time Leon was here and the machine just died. I'm sure you know what I mean."

"Yes, sir. I do. That was a tragedy. I lost a lot of friends on that mission."

The General nodded. "As did I. Do you think the hanger will be alright with you gone for a while? I'm fine with you leaving some of your people topside to man essential services."

"It should be, if I can leave a skeleton crew up here. I've trained some of the best people for the job, and they'll be more than capable in my absence."

"Sounds, good. Now, go get yourself outfitted."

"Yes, sir," said Jim, saluting again, and then he sprinted off in the direction of the weapons room.

A short time later, Jerry was in full battle gear as he strode in front of the crew with the Remi rifle at port arms, into the briefing room. He saluted the General and walked to the front of the room.

"I know some of you have heard of this rifle already. And, some of you have seen it demonstrated. But today is the day you're all going to learn how to fire and maintain it," Jerry said.

Leon and the General smiled at each other and the General patted his Remi. There were a dozen men on the work crew who were clearly not soldiers. They were brought in from the civilian world for their tunnel boring expertise with the big drills.

Maybe that was part of the problem last time; too many engineers and not enough soldiers. Here we go again...

But that thought would soon vanish from Leon's mind. As the capabilities of the new weapon were demonstrated, a group of ten soldiers entered the room and stood at the back of the class.

"Nice of you folks to join us. Sorry, there aren't any more seats," Jerry said. "But I'll be brief, and then we'll hit the range."

The officer in command of the ten men nodded at Jerry, "That's fine. Please, continue and I apologize for our lateness. We had our own last-minute briefing to finish up," the Special Forces Commander said.

The General turned in his seat to look at the troops who had just entered and gave a salute to the Commander. He wondered what *that* briefing was all about, and would be sure to ask after the firing range duties were done.

Jerry showed them all the basic functions of the new rifle, and its counterpart; the Remi EPP, a pistol. Both were plasma energy beam weapons capable of a single shot pulse, or adjustable auto fire of several pulses of plasma energy per second. The effects, Jerry promised, were devastating and would be shown shortly. He ran them through the operations of the weapons and how to change the settings. After that, he asked if anyone had any questions.

"I do," said one of the soldiers who had come in with the Commander. "What about cleaning? Are you going into that?"

"There's nothing to clean, or maintain. Since the weapons fire only energy, there are no deposits left in the barrels, or anywhere else."

There was stunned silence for a moment, then the room erupted in murmurs from the curious and disbelieving soldiers, who had been trained to clean and break down their weapons on a regular basis. It would take a bit of adjustment for them to get used to the new paradigm, but once they did, they would be very pleased with their new guns.

"Come on, let's go out to the range, then you can really see what I'm talking about!" said Jerry. The group got up with a commotion and filed out to the firing range.

The range was located underground at the base, but only one level down, nowhere near the tunnels; it didn't even have direct access to the tunnels, so Leon felt safe there. Jerry had a couple of soldiers help him to move a pallet of the new weapons to the range, and get them unpacked. The new guns gleamed in the overhead florescent lights.

Once everyone had a rifle, and a pistol, Jerry smiled, "Ok, it's just like firing an ordinary gun, in that the kick will still be there, but it will be a lot less. The main thing you will notice, apart from lack of any gun smoke smell, is the lack of sound. There's a slight buzzing noise as they ramp up, and then when you fire, there's a "pulsing" sound, but no big bangs. Sorry folks, if you were expecting that, and I know that the "bangs" can be a psychological weapon, but these are much different guns, and I think you will agree, superior."

"So much for firing a warning shot that will scare them off," one of the recruits piped up.

"Oh, the flash from one of these will scare off most people, and especially Greys, plenty!" Jerry laughed. "Well, enough of my yakking. Take 'em for a test drive!"

Each man got into position at his own firing booth and aimed at the targets down range. First, plasma bursts shot out of a couple of guns, fired with trepidation, then all of the guns erupted in a near-blinding flashes and barrages of blue energy beams. The targets were soon only smoking husks.

"Nice gun," said Leon. "I'm looking forward to giving those Grey bastards some payback!" He tilted the gun sideways, looking it over.

Jerry stopped by Leon and peered into his booth. "Heh! That's the spirit! Let's go kick some Grey butt!" laughed Jerry.

From the entrance door to the firing range stepped Frank, Leon's crew mate from the last trip down in the tunnels.

"Hey, Frank!" Leon put down his rifle, and left his firing position to greet his friend. "How are you doing?"

"Surviving. It's good to see you," Frank smiled as they shook hands.

"You too, man! You just get back here?"

"Yeah, I had some loose ends to tie up at home, but guess what, I'm back, too!"

"Well, I'm glad you are. It's good to have a familiar face around when you're underground.

Frank looked at the new guns. "These are neat! I'm here to learn how to use them."

"Well, let's get you started then," said Jerry. He handed Frank a rifle and started to run him through its paces.

15

The night before he was to go back underground, Leon poked around on the laptop in his room to distract his thoughts from the coming day. He looked around on the secret military darknet, but his access was quite restricted, so the really interesting things he wanted to see, like the files on the aliens and the secret space program, were denied him.

"Dammit!" He turned off the machine.

One day, I'll get to see all of that and really know what's going on!

Then, he lay in the dark, wondering if maybe that was really driving his continuing work with the secret military: his curiosity to *know*, beyond his desire for revenge. He had always been the curious type and liked to know how things worked. Why should knowing about how the world *really* worked be any different?

He turned on the light and spent some time looking at his wounded hand. It had healed up and didn't hurt much anymore. He had even learned how to work around its limitations. Still, he'd give a lot to be whole again. He ran his hand across his chest, feeling the rough scars under his shirt from his last encounter underground with the Greys.

He glanced over at the new rifle propped up in the corner and wondered if he really wanted to go back down there, even if it meant he could get some revenge. He might get into even more trouble, or killed this time. But he'd had those thoughts thousands of times lately, so he pushed them out of his mind. He turned on some calming music and did some deep breathing to relax. Eventually, he lay down and fell asleep.

Such thoughts gave way to restless dreams, and he awoke several times during the night, sweating, with images of Greys in his head, and yelling out "No!" and "Stop!" He just hoped he hadn't been loud enough to upset anyone else.

He awoke early and welcomed the light of dawn through the window. It might be the last light he'd see for a while, or ever, again, so he savored it, drinking a cup of coffee alone in his room, looking out the window.

After breakfast, Leon and the rest of the team were ordered to the briefing room. The General went over the facts: their mission was to open up the tunnel again, at the scene of the Grey's attack, enter their cavern outpost, and if any Greys were still there, then force them back on a retreat. Once the area was secured they were to gather intelligence and see what they could find. After that, the Grey's maglev system was going to be explored. Another mission would attach robotically controlled maglev cars to it, and send them far into the Grey's tunnel system to learn more about what they were doing.

It was mainly an exploration mission, and Leon wondered why he was even going along, but he knew that his expertise would be needed if there was a tunnel cave-in, or they needed to dig an emergency way out of the Grey's tunnel. He wasn't looking forward to another possible shoot out, but if there was one, then he might have his revenge. His hand found the grip of his handgun and he held onto it tightly.

The General had added some new men to the team. They were all introduced, but the stress made Leon forget most of their names instantly.

"How are you feeling, Leon? Ready to get back down there?" the General put a hand on Leon's shoulder, making him jump and shaking him out of his daydreaming.

"I guess so. As ready as I can ever be," he forced a smile.

"That's what I like to hear!"

"Do you think we're doing the right thing?"

"What? Going into the Grey's tunnel? We've got to flush them out and see how far their network has advanced, see how it's going to impact our further tunneling. I thought you understood the wisdom in that?" the General tightened his lips and stared at Leon, starting to think he was losing his nerve. He knew how hard it could be for a man to get back down into the tunnels after something like Leon had been through.

"That's all fine. I mean, can we not just divert our own tunnels? Just close up the Grey's tunnels, and go our own way?"

The General shook his crew cut head, "It would never work. We need to close down their operations there, or they'll be all over us constantly. I've seen them at work for a long time, believe me. You'll be fine. You're going in with a great group, and you've got some really nice, new gear."

"Yeah, I suppose," Leon shrugged.

Of course, he's not going down there with us!

"Are you coming down, too?"

"If my schedule allows, I may make an appearance." The General clapped Leon's shoulder and walked off, hoping he was not sending him and the others to their deaths.

That figures.

The General brought a new man up to the front, "Folks, this is your Sergeant for the mission, John Maxwell." He was big, tough, and military all the way, a career man who had seen plenty of action in his fifty-plus years on Earth, most of those in the service. He would be leading them down into the tunnels.

***

The ride down to the tunnels was one of the longest of Leon's life, even though it only lasted a few minutes. Frank and Leon looked at each other in the elevator and tried to smile, but they both had fear and sadness in their eyes. None of the others had been with them last time they were in the tunnels and attacked, so Leon knew they could not fully understand what it had been like.

"Ok, everyone, look alive. Keep 'em locked and clocked at all times, we are in hostile territory!" shouted Maxwell.

Leon checked his guns and made sure they were both ready, even though he'd been over them many times that morning. But he checked again and made sure that the new REMI laser rifle was good to go at a moments notice. He gripped it tightly, his hands starting to sweat.

The elevator came to a smooth stop, and he felt his stomach return to normal. Everyone unbuckled and moved out.

The empty elevator went back to the surface. Then, a few minutes later, the elevator arrived with the rest of the crew. Leon was glad they had more men with them this time, especially more soldiers.

"Damn shame, eh? All the folks that died down here?" It was Perry, one of the new recruits, probably no more than twenty years old.

"It is. It was pretty terrible," Leon raised his wounded hand and showed it to the kid.

"Oh, geez! You were down here the first time! I'm sorry, man. I didn't know!"

"That's ok. Don't worry about it," Leon smiled. "We'll get those Greys this time."

"Saddle up, folks!" Maxwell shouted. "We're ready to move out." He gestured to the cars on the maglev tracks. The cars wobbled around as the men got on, loading the cars to their maximum weight, and maybe a little over it.

Leon walked over to one of cars, with thoughts of his family going through his head, and the sun, and wide open spaces that he wondered if he'd ever seen again.

"You think these things are safe with all this weight?" Frank half-joked.

"I don't think anything is safe down here anymore, but too late for that, huh?" Leon said.

"Got that right!"

We must be nuts for coming down here again. Maybe we have a death wish. Just admit it, Leon. Nothing wrong with a little revenge, besides!

He gripped his rifle tighter and climbed aboard the second maglev car, which was already cramped, willing the dark thoughts out of his head. He was starting to sweat.

"Leon! Not in that one. I want you up here," called out Maxwell, leaning out the door of the first car.

"Go on, I'll hang back here," Frank said.

"Shit," Leon said and got up to leave the car. He got in the first car. Most of the others had their helmets off and were sweating, too. He didn't feel so self-conscious then, and took off his helmet, also.

"Damn hot down in some of these tunnels, huh?" smiled Perry.

"Don't worry, it'll cool off some as soon as we get underway," said Leon.

"Ah, good," Perry nodded.

"Perry, let Leon sit there," Maxwell pointed at the seat near the front windshield.

Maxwell was at the controls of the first car and once he saw that everyone was aboard he closed the doors, waiting until the seals around the doors pressurized themselves before moving the car. "Thanks, Leon. I thought it best that you ride up here in the first car. That way, if there are any tunnel anomalies, you'll get first look."

"Right, good idea," Leon nodded. It was true, but it was also true that the first car would be in the front line for any trouble. He was starting to feel ill. The wounds on his hand and chest throbbed, even though they were quite healed. He felt an overall apprehension, and most of his thoughts, except those of fear, were starting to be drowned out by his pounding heart and throbbing temples. He felt a headache coming on.

Maxwell energized the maglev car and it came to life with a slight shudder that settled into a steady hum. He moved the throttle forward and the car started to glide along, with a completely smooth movement.

Leon was still amazed by the vehicle. He was actually starting to enjoy himself, as air started to blow through the car, its movement making it slightly cooler, and the AC kicking in.

The headlights of the first maglev illuminated the tunnel ahead, reflecting off the smooth walls. It seemed to Leon like he was going on a subway ride – or maybe into Disney's Space Mountain.

Except for the aliens!

He leaned over to look at the controls, to distract himself. The speed indicator climbed steadily and settled at just under 100 miles per hour.

"We can go a lot faster, of course, but I'm going to keep it down in case we come across anything...undesirable. We'll have a hard time getting stopped quickly if we're at max speed," said the Sergeant. "Plus, we've got a full load."

Leon looked at the red line speed and it topped out at 800 miles per hour. "Can this thing really go that fast?" Leon marveled.

"Sure. With no friction from the tracks, it's much easier to gain and maintain that sort of speed. And, most of the tunnels down here are straight lines, so it's safe to crank the cars up. Usually, the only traffic down here is ours. Sonic booms occur around 768 miles per hour, so we've got to be aware of that if we're running under any inhabited areas, depending on the depth of the tunnel, and the strata, of course."

"My God!" Leon looked over the screens on the control panel and noticed a radar scope. The maglev car was sending out a radar ping, and he watched its return and the graphics the screen drew. So far it was clear ahead.

He settled back in his seat and looked around at the others. Most of them looked fairly comfortable, veterans of underground maglev transport. Except for Perry, who looked nervous, and gripped his gun with a white-knuckled grip.

"Easy, Perry! We're running cool, here," Leon said.

"T-thanks, but this is my first time underground."

"Nothing to it. I've been down here so many times, it's like a second home; I used to be a civilian contractor before joining up with this group."

"Oh, yeah?"

"Sure, nothing to it."

"Oh, ok. If you say so," Perry gulped, looking at the stumps of Leon's severed fingers.

The second maglev car followed along at a respectable distance, leaving some extra space in case of the need for an emergency stop. Leon looked back and watched its headlights glittering into the car he was in. The motion of the vehicle was relaxing, the sound of the air hissing by lulled him. And, with nothing to do, it was enough to make his eyelids feel heavy and he found himself starting to drift off – but he soon jerked wide awake when he remembered the situation he was in.

"Look alive, Verdat! We've got bogeys coming up," said Maxwell, pointing to a blob growing larger on the radar scope, as the screen started beeping.

"Any idea what it is?" Leon sat up.

"Not yet, but we'll know soon." Maxwell touched his helmet microphone, clicking it on. "Car 2, you see that?"

"Roger, coming up fast, twelve o'clock," said a voice from the second car, reproduced over Maxwell's earphones, and echoed in the earphones of everyone's helmets.

The scanners that each soldier had all went off, beeping wildly, making a big racket in the car.

"Turn those things to silent!" Maxwell shouted. The beepings died down one by one as they turned their scanners to silent mode. "Reducing speed," Maxwell said into his microphone. He eased the throttle back and the car still moved forward with no apparent loss of speed for a few moments, so efficient was the magnetic, frictionless suspension. Soon though, the car began to slow. The object on the radar scope grew larger and the scope continued to beep out a steady warning, getting faster and faster.

"This could be it folks. Safeties off!" commanded Maxwell.

Leon saw everyone check their weapons and switch their safety to off. The headlights of the car behind them began to fall back.

Perry wiped his forehead with his sleeve, looking very scared. The warning signal began to beep faster and faster.

"Don't worry, kid. You only die once," one of the soldiers quipped to Perry.

"Gee, thanks," Perry said.

The soldier offered him some chewing gum.

Leon looked at Perry, "We're not gonna let anything happen to us without a fight."

The lead maglev came to a stop at the end of the tracks and the doors hissed open. Warmer air blew into the car, along with a scent of damp earth. Everyone was on their feet at once and stepped out of the car, rifles at the ready. Ahead of them was the new tunnel, going on for maybe a mile. The maglev tracks had been extended since Leon had last been down, and went nearly to the end of the tunnel he had been digging when they were attacked.

There were a few temporary work lights stuck on the walls, ending at the stranded tunnel boring machine. Leon recognized it at once; he swallowed hard as he saw the scene of the last battle. Beyond that was solid rock and earth, in darkness. A few Humvees stood waiting.

The second maglev stopped and all the soldiers got out, coming to stand near the first team, looking around, rifles pointing into the darkness. They loaded into the Humvees and drove fast to the end of the tunnel ahead. The scanners in the Humvees showed many Greys beyond the end of the tunnel, coming up. Some of the soldiers checked their own hand-held scanners and were getting the same readings, the screens lighting up their faces in the darkened cabins.

The Humvees stopped in front of the stranded boring machine. There were no Greys in sight. The soldiers got out, then the Humvees were turned around so that they were facing back the way they had come, in case they needed to make a fast retreat.

Leon looked around, feeling great apprehension at coming back to the spot where he had nearly been killed. Some of the dirt was stained with human blood, and black alien blood.

Perry walked to the covered over hole in the tunnel wall. "W-what's in here?"

Maxwell turned to the group. "That's the hole the Greys made, that was sealed up last time. We are at the edge of a Grey base. They probably know we're here already, so look alive. In fact, I'd bet on it. Johnson, bring the cutter!"

One of the troops brought a larger rifle-type device forward. It was on a tripod and had a screen on the top. Johnson aimed it at the patched up tunnel wall, centering the patch in the crosshairs on the screen.

Maxwell peered at the screen, making some adjustments to the controls. He watched as the radar brought back images beyond their tunnel wall. "Ok, looks clear. Do it!"

Johnson nodded and fired up the cutter. It came to life with a loud whine. He pressed the button and a fat, blue laser beam shot out of the barrel, melting the tunnel wall where it hit.

"Everyone back!" Maxwell shouted over the noise of the rock being disintegrated and popping.

Johnson expertly moved the cutter around, making a smoking outline in the rock, then he shut the beam off. Maxwell went up to the smoking outline, kicked it, and it fell into an open space beyond. He poked his head in and saw a large, open cavern before him. It was illuminated by glowing moss on many of the rocks in the area. In the distance, he saw a bunch of Greys milling around in front of a black, hive-like building. They were just standing there, staring, waiting for them.

"Oh, shit," Frank said, holding his nose, nudging Leon's shoulder. It was the stench of the Greys, again, quickly flowing in from the hole.

Leon was going pale, but was determined to give the aliens some payback. He covered his nose with his sleeve and took some deep breaths, straightening up.

"What the hell is that stink?" Perry gagged, stepping away from the hole. He dry-heaved, bent over double.

"Aliens, son. Prepare to engage!" Maxwell looked over his troops and nodded.

Perry kept backing away, stepping on the boots of those behind him.

"Perry! This is not the time for this kind of thing!" Maxwell scolded him.

"I, w-want to get out of here," Perry was starting to scramble back to the Humvee. Maxwell grabbed him by the arm.

"Get back here, soldier! Do you want to be court-marshaled? Or, maybe we'll just lock you up down here, forever. How'd you like that?" Maxwell's eyes were bulging out of his head.

Perry started to make sounds like he was crying.

Then, the tunnel wall next to the newly cut hole was blasted outwards by a large green laser blast. Leon, Frank and the others were thrown to the ground, as pieces of rock and dirt rained down on them. Laser blasts kept coming from the other side of the broken tunnel wall, through the smoke and dust.

"Goddammit! There goes our element of surprise!" Maxwell yelled. "On your feet!"

Dozens of large heads, with almond shaped eyes and small, wiry bodies stepped out of the hole, firing on them; the Greys.

The Lord is my shepherd, he protecth me...

Leon prayed as he rolled over in the dirt, got behind a pile of rubble and started returning fire on the Greys, wasting no time on his revenge. Grey heads popped open in sprays of black blood and goo, as he cut them apart with shots from his new laser rifle.

He heard a cry behind him, and looked back to see Perry fall down with several holes in his armour and helmet where the Greys had hit them with their deadly green lasers.

The tunnel was lit up brightly with the multitude of laser blasts from the Greys and humans, trading back and forth in different colours, and getting fewer and fewer, as combatants fell on both sides.

Leon was not as shocked as some of the others were, as he'd seen the Greys before. But many of the men were in disbelief of what they were seeing and were ineffective. The Greys picked them off easily. But Leon and the few experienced fighters made up for the difference, killing many Greys between them.

Maxwell crouched beside Leon and fired at the aliens. "Damn lot of them!" Maxwell shouted.

Leon just grunted "Yeah," as he was too busy shooting and picking off Grays to say much.

A big Grey, larger than the rest, had a translucent shield covering its body, and the laser blasts just bounced off it. That Grey, probably the commander and a higher life-form than the more robotic, smaller Greys, stood at the back, watching the smaller Greys fall in front of it, then it retreated when too many of them started to be killed.

Leon, Maxwell, and a handful of the troops remaining managed to hold the Greys off, keeping them at bay. Then, suddenly, the laser blasts from the Greys stopped; they just turned and ran, all together, back into the hole they had come from.

Maxwell looked at the scanner and saw that the Greys were retreating fast, beyond the hole. He stood up and looked around at all of the fallen humans, mixed in with alien bodies. "We've taken a lot of hits" he said into his microphone. "We've got them on the run boys, good job! Now, let's tend to our wounded. Leon, you and Frank cover that hole." The groans of wounded men could be heard from various places in the tunnel.

Frank dusted himself off. He'd been shielding himself behind a Humvee, and he was fine, but the machine had numerous holes in it from the alien's rays.

Leon waved Frank over to a position on either side of the hole.

"Thank God we're ok!" Leon said.

"I can't believe how crazy that was!" Frank looked through the hole with wide eyes, watching the remaining Greys, maybe ten of them, running back to their base, with the taller leader far in the distance. "Think they'll be back?" He fired after them, hitting a couple in the back, sending them down.

"I dunno. Maybe not for a while. Seems we spooked them." Leon checked his scanner and saw no aliens in the immediate area beyond the hole. He stuck his head in the hole, "Looks like they're running scared." He saw a vast cavern, and a maglev system with train cars much like their own, in fact, they had probably copied it from the aliens, he was starting to think. Grey bodies littered the area just beyond the hole. In the distance he saw a structure, low, with a couple of windows. It was black, and resembled a hornet's nest.

He fired at the running Greys, but they were getting out of range.

Just then a massive explosion came from deep within the Grey's cavern: BA-BOOM! The sound made the men hit the ground and it echoed through the tunnel.

"What the hell was that?" Maxwell came to the hole and looked inside. Dirt rained down in the distance, at the far end of Grey's cavern. They had blown up their own tunnel with the maglev line, sealing the tunnel behind them as they escaped on their maglev cars. There would be no following them that way, at least not until they could dig it out. Some of the windows in their building were now blown out, and black smoke was billowing out of them.

Maxwell whistled. "I'll be damned! They blew up their own stuff so we couldn't follow them. Damn strange, sight, huh?"

Leon got back up and looked though the hole, "My, God!"

Frank stuck his head through the hole, too. "Holy shit!"

"Sneaky bastards!" Maxwell said.

"So, we're just letting them get away?" Leon asked.

"For now. What else can we do? You want to dig that out with your bare hands?" Maxwell snickered and took off his helmet, wiped his sweaty head with his sleeve. "But, we'll get them. Don't you worry. We'll get that tunnel dug out and track them down," he stared at the smoking ruins in the distance, shaking his head, "I didn't know the little bastards had it in them."

A voice on the radio spoke: "We felt that rumble up here. Report status. Over."

Maxwell leaned back into the main tunnel and clicked on his com, "The bogeys are on the run and have abandoned their post. We have several wounded and several dead. I'll evac the wounded, now. Then, after I've secured the area, we'll extract. Over."

"Roger that," said the voice on the radio.

"Help me load up, then we can take a closer look at those buildings," Maxwell said, pointing his gun at the alien station. Leon and Frank looked at each other, then into the hole.

Once all of the wounded were loaded in a Humvee, it tore off down the tunnel, back to the maglev.

Leon found it particularity difficult to load the bodies of the dead onto another Humvee, including that of young Perry.

It could have been me, so easily!

Once all of the bodies were aboard, Maxwell closed up the Humvee and it left, too. They stood there, watching the vehicles speed away from them, their lights illuminating the tunnel, until they were gone.

Silence grew in the tunnel and Leon turned to Frank, "Eerie, isn't it? To know that we are here, miles underground, with those Greys?"

Frank nodded, "Yeah. I'd rather it was large, monster rats!"

Leon looked around at the new, red blood stains in the tunnel, and the still-wet pools of black blood, and splatter on the walls.

Maxwell set his feet in a wide stance in the dirt and glanced through the hole in the tunnel. "I think we should take a look at their outpost before we seal this tunnel up. They left in a hurry, so they might have left some tech that we can use, or clues as to where they went. We might get some good intel."

"You think that's a good idea going into their lair?" Leon peered at the smoking alien building.

"They're long gone! Look at the place!" Maxwell lit a cigarette, puffing smoke.

"But, what about booby traps? Is it safe to go in there?" Frank asked, biting his lip.

"Sure!" Maxwell bellowed. "Those cockroaches don't use booby traps. I've never seen them use any kind of trap yet, but we'll be careful. It should be fine. I'll hold your hand; I've seen this kind of thing before. Come on, I'll lead the way!" Maxwell stepped through the hole and entered the alien's cavern.

Frank turned to Leon. "What, now?"

"Want to check out their building?"

"Not really, but I don't want any nasty surprises following us out."

"You got that right!"

"I hope we're not being stupid."

"Would you rather wait here?"

"No! Let's go!" Frank whispered.

They stepped through the opening and into the cavern. It was not nearly as dark in there as the tunnel had been, as there was luminous fungus everywhere, giving the tunnel an eerie, green glow. Still, they kept the lights on their helmets switched on, and also the lights on top of their guns.

Maxwell was a short distance inside, holding the scanner in front of him as he walked. It didn't register anything living in the area ahead. He swept it around in circles, making sure there were no Greys hiding in hidden places in the walls of the cavern, or in any of the small sheds that were scattered around. Black smoke drifted out of shattered buildings, and there was the smell of smoke and burnt, putrid Grey flesh in the air; the Greys had a bad smell already, and burning them only made it worse. Grey bodies trailed on the ground, leading to the base.

Step by cautious step, they came to the Grey's main building. The structure looked like a hornet's nest, black, and made of rings rising to a peak. It appeared to be made of metal, but was not reflective. There were windows, small and rectangular, on the top level. Several of them were blown out in hanging shards, with thick, black smoke still pouring out, and black soot covering the exterior surfaces around the window frames. The entrance door was no more than four feet high and it was closed. There was no handle, just a small indentation in the metal, suitable for alien fingers to grasp. It looked to be made of a reinforced metal, like a blast door, and it was locked, not giving when Maxwell pushed, or pulled on it, cramping his fingers into the indentation. He wiped his fingers off on his pant leg after.

There was a back door to the structure and it was open. Maxwell stood at the door, waiting for them, hanging off to the side. He moved the scanner around and it registered nothing. Leon and Frank walked as quietly as they could towards the door, their rifles gripped tight and pointed into the semi-darkness, the light beams from their helmets and guns breaking the gloom within. Maxwell nodded and they entered, ducking down to clear the doorframe.

They were able to stand up in the hallway, with its higher ceiling. It stunk in there, of Greys and burning, and made their faces scrunch up until they got used to it. As their eyes adjusted, the first thing they noticed was that the inside was lit with low, green, indirect lights, very easy on the eyes. Leon thought that must be due to the Grey's large eyes, as they were probably sensitive to bright lights. The walls were made of the same material as the outside of the structure, as far as they could tell, with black, metallic ribbing to give it strength; it looked biomechanical, like the inside of an evil whale. Symbols were on the walls at various points, in the Grey's language, which none of them could read.

They walked down the hallway. The air was getting cooler, the further they moved inside. Thick smoke reached their noses, making them cough.

A Grey streaked across the hallway, freezing them all in their tracks.

"Shit!" Frank yelled.

Then they ran after it, shooting, until they tore it to pieces. Its remains lay in a black, bloody pool on the floor.

"That's weird," Maxwell said, stepping over the dead alien, "they usually all go together when they run. And, the scanner didn't go off. Very strange. Keep your eyes open!" He looked down the corridor where the alien had been running, his rifle held out straight. Beads of sweat had started on his forehead.

Leon looked at him, wondering if they were really walking into a death trap. "I thought you said this place was empty," he whispered to Maxwell.

"I thought it was."

"Then how come our scanners didn't pick that one up?"

"Look, I dunno," Maxwell shrugged. "What, you want to go back yourself, now? Too late. We'll all leave together after we've checked this place out. So, just chill out and keep alert." Maxwell kept creeping forward.

Leon looked to Frank, who nodded. They kept following Maxwell, as the alternative of going back alone was not very appealing, either.

The dead alien had fallen in front of a door, its hand reaching for it. Maxwell pointed to the door, and they got against the wall, to either side of the door. He counted down from three to one, silently, mouthing the words, then pulled the door open.

Nothing moved inside.

Maxwell dipped his head low in the doorframe, then out again. Still, nothing.

He only saw a room, with low lighting and no movement within. He jumped inside, hit the floor and rolled off to the side behind some metal boxes.

Still nothing.

Waiting a few seconds, he peeked his head over the cases and called out, "Ok, you two, get in here. It's clear."

Frank and Leon stepped inside. Leon found what looked like a light switch on the wall and touched it. Overhead lights came to life in the room.

What they found there was like a waking nightmare.

They saw hundreds of people of all races in transparent containers, frozen, and most of them were children.

"What the hell?" Maxwell gasped.

Off to one side was a stainless steel table, with grooves in the sides, like an autopsy table. A collection of knives and automated cutting tools were above it, suspended, ready for use.

"What's this? A morgue?" Leon asked.

"They don't eat humans, do they?" Frank's eyes were wide, like he was on the edge of panic.

"I've never heard of this before," Maxwell went over to one of the containers. He touched the frosty glass. It was very cold.

Leon and Frank stood staring at the bodies in the tanks, trying to make some sense out of it, but all they got was more horrified at the sight.

Maxwell flipped on the radio, "Control, we're got a situation down here. Do you read?" But, the only response he got was static. "The radio isn't working. We better get out of here, right away. Come on." He tugged at Leon's shoulder.

"We can't just leave them here!" Leon cried out, turning away from the tanks.

"What do you want to do? They'll all dead!" Maxwell hissed.

"Shouldn't we get the bodies out of here, so they can he identified? I'm sure their families would like to know," Leon fixed a hard stare at him.

"Know what? That their son or daughter, their baby, was killed by aliens and was being stored, frozen, in an underground base when we found them? A base that just happened to intersect one of our own secret, underground bases? What are you talking about?" Maxwell shook his head. "We don't have the equipment to get them out now, even if we wanted to. We'll have to come back another time. The top brass will want us to get them out, don't worry. But, we can't do it now. Let's go; I've seen enough."

Leon tried to say something, but just opened and shut his mouth.

Maxwell made sure he got a few pictures of the containers with a small, pocket camera, then he moved towards to the door, "Let's get the fuck out of here!"

Frank and Leon followed him down the hallway. They walked back out of the building, looking around franticly, their rifles at the ready. But, they made it back out without incident.

Maxwell trudged forward ahead of them, "Move it! I don't like the looks of this place."

Leon took out his scanner and waved it around in a circle. "Nothing," he said. "Just Maxwell, up ahead," pointing to a blip on the screen which displayed Maxwell's name next to it. The scanner was picking up an ID that Maxwell was carrying, or a microchip implant, he was not sure which, but he wouldn't put a microchip out of the question at this point, after all he'd experienced recently.

"If we can trust those scanners, anymore," Frank said. "How come we didn't pick up that Grey that we met in there?"

"Maybe there was some shielding in the building."

Frank and Leon followed Maxwell back across the cavern floor, stepping over more dead alien bodies.

"Control, do you read me?" Maxwell kept trying his radio, until he finally got a response.

"Control here. Go ahead."

"We're on our way back out. Radio transmission failed for a while there. I suspect they had jammers in the vicinity of their structures. We'll need a large extraction team for this location. We found many human bodies stored here. I'll tell you more when we get back. Over."

"Roger that."

Once they got back into their own tunnel, Maxwell aimed the gun on the tripod to a spot above the hole in the wall.

"Get back, you two," he shouted, waiting until Leon and Frank were out of the way. He fired and the rock started to melt and slide down over the hole, forming a hard seal.

He carried the tripod back to the Humvee and they all got aboard.

The three men sat, not talking, listening to the noises of the Humvee, and watching the walls of the tunnel speed by. Leon wondered what Mary and Jennie were doing now.

After they got back to the surface, Maxwell took Leon and Frank into a meeting room for a short debriefing. He recorded their conversation, but it was nothing but a formality. Maxwell would produce a detailed written report later. He kept the meeting short, as he seemed just as anxious as Leon and Frank to wrap up the day's events. They all just wanted to go home, but that would not be possible until they had received a formal debriefing from the General, and possibly they would have to help recover the bodies.

Leon called his wife and dearly wished he could speak about what had happened, as it would ease his mind, but he could not. "Hi, it's me. I hope I didn't wake you."

"No. Are you ok?" She heard the edge in his voice.

"I'm...doing ok. How's things at home?" He felt surreal asking her a question like that, after what he'd just seen.

"We're fine. When are you coming home?"

"As soon as I can, honey. As soon as I can."

It was hard to get off the phone with her, and made him miss her and Jennie, and home, even more.

***

After he'd showered, got a change of clothes, and something to eat, Leon felt much better. But he still wanted to get outside.

It had snowed lightly, the air much colder in the elevation of the high desert, and he walked a short distance from the door of the base to look at the full moon shining down, making the snow sparkle and glow slightly blue. He was glad to be outside, and sighed in the cool, night air. His breath was visible and it rose up in a plume, quickly dissipating. The moon was so bright that it cast shadows from the bare branches of the trees and overhanging wires onto the snow below. He thought it would be bright enough to read by. It was so beautiful out there, and quiet.

Romantic. If only Mary could see this.

Tears came to his eyes. He was so happy to be alive and just wanted to go home.

16

Leon stepped back inside the base and felt the warmth creeping back into his face and hands. He found Maxwell and Frank sitting around in the kitchen having coffee, both too freaked out to sleep.

"Join the insomnia club," Maxwell handed Leon a mug.

"Thanks," he said and poured himself a cup. He knew he wasn't going to get any sleep that night, anyway.

"How are you feeling?" Frank asked.

"Do I look that rough?" Leon joked.

"I think this thing has been rough on all of us," Maxwell said, then fell silent. The images of the frozen people, especially the children, were still vivid in their minds, and would probably be for the rest of their lives.

"Are the Greys from a distant future?" Leon asked. "That's what I heard. Maybe they're time travelers, with all that advanced technology?" He had been listening to late night talk radio, like Art Bell for years, and there were many theories going around about what the Greys actually were. He had thought they were all just stories, until very recently.

"We're not sure," Maxwell turned to him. "They've been here for a lot longer than us. They have advanced technology, yes. Can they time travel? I don't know. But, whether all the technology they have was their own ingenuity, or they got it from somewhere else, is up for debate. If you ask me, I think they got it from somewhere, or someone; they don't seem that bright to me."

Leon thought it over. The aliens *did* seem advanced to him, if not pleasing to the eye, or nose. "What about their structures? Those seemed pretty innovative."

Maxwell waved his hand. "Naw, you ever see an ant hive? That's innovative. These Greys have been doing the same things for years and years, nothing changes."

Leon felt that Maxwell was not telling him everything, but that was just business as usual, he was finding out, working on secret military projects.

Why change, when quality doesn't go out of style?

Leon sighed, "In light of all that's happened, am I still expected to fulfill my contract? I could use some time off right about now."

Frank looked from Leon to Maxwell. "Me too," he said.

Maxwell looked at them both, in turn. "Fellas, that's not in my hands. But, I'll see what I can do. It was a hell of a thing we went through. I expect that there will be some delays and reorganizing in the tunnel boring operations. We've got to deal with the wounded, lay the dead to rest, and then assemble a new crew to get those bodies out. Then, we have to plan how to dig out that Grey tunnel. I don't think you'll be needed for anything soon. As far as I'm concerned, you might as well go home for a while. I'll put in a word for you both."

"Thanks."

Frank nodded, "Yeah, thanks."

"Sure thing. If you two feel you'd like to talk to someone, we've got good shrinks on staff. Just say the word." With that, Maxwell stood up. "Well, I am going to at least *try* and get some rest. That was a job well done, both of you. You should be proud." He shook both their hands and left them alone in the kitchen, with the whirring of the fans to take up the quiet of the otherwise deserted room.

The next morning, Leon and Frank went to visit the wounded in the hospital wing and spread what cheer they could. Leon was especially inspiring, as he had survived an alien attack in the past and the crew looked up to him.

Next, each surviving man from the mission was debriefed privately by the General, and it was all recorded.

After they all had finished, Maxwell joined them and gave them the good news. "You've been cleared to go home. Here are your papers." Maxwell smiled and handed Leon and Frank envelopes. "And, a nice bonus."

They took their envelopes with bittersweet thoughts. Sure, it was nice to get a big, fat paycheque, and a bonus, too, but at what cost? Both of them would never be the same again, and some of the others were not even going home. They shook Maxwell's hand, then went back to their rooms to change out of their uniforms and pack.

That evening, Leon, Frank, and some of the other survivors said goodbye to the General, then got into limos to take them all home. Frank and Leon shared a limo, as they lived nearby each other, but they mainly slept on the ride home, as they were still so exhausted from the mission.

***

Hours later, in the morning, the limo dropped Leon at the parking lot of his business, and Frank stepped out to say goodbye.

"Let's stay in touch, ok?" Leon said. "It would be good to have someone to talk to, who I can relate to."

"I know what you mean. Yeah, sure, fuck the regulations!" Frank ginned and shook Leon's good hand. He got back into the limo and slammed the door.

Leon watched the limo move off, smiling to himself; at least he had met a true friend in all this mess. He sighed and got into his SUV.

17

It was early morning when Leon got home. He stopped for a coffee on the way to steady his nerves. Mary had taken the day off to greet him, and get caught up, and their daughter Jennie was in school.

Getting back home the second time was even harder on him. Being in his wife's arms again felt so good, and the memories that flooded his mind of what he'd just been through were so bad, that it was a very strange push and pull of emotions.

There was so much he wanted to be able to tell his wife and friends, but he had been sworn to secrecy. He was not sure it was worth it anymore to keep the secrets, but was afraid of what the consequences might be if he broke his contract. What would happen to his family? To him?

And, what would he do if they wanted him to come back to work on another secret job? He didn't know if he'd ever be able to go back into those tunnels, again. But, when he thought of those people, those children in the freezers, he knew he had to do something to stop the Greys. If that was continuing to work with the secret military, then that's what he'd do. But, that day had not yet come, and might never come, so he just wanted to take some time to get back to his regular life.

Leon and his wife drove to pick up Jennie from school, and she nearly exploded with excitement when she saw her father was behind the wheel. She jumped into the SUV and almost strangled Leon when she hugged him in his seat. He laughed and hugged her back, telling her how glad he was to see her. Finally, she calmed down enough that she could buckle herself in.

He took them to a drive-through and they had a quick bite to eat before heading off for the rest of the afternoon in the country. They went to a small town and enjoyed walking around together, looking at the cute shops and quaint décor. His family didn't ask much about what he'd been doing, as they were getting used to the fact that he couldn't talk about it.

He tried to get caught up on their lives instead, and found that he'd missed a fair bit; school plays, high scores on tests, and walks through the big piles of leaves that had collected on the sides of the streets. He was sorry about that and resolved to make it up to them, and not to miss so much in the future, particularly of his young daughter's life.

Sitting out on his back porch that evening, enjoying the setting sun after a nice day with his family, he searched his soul. He did a lot of looking out into the distance without saying much, but his mind was working overtime.

His wife noticed something was troubling him and took his hand, "What's wrong? There's been something on your mind since you came back, I can tell."

He grimaced and slugged back the last of his iced tea. He swatted a mosquito from his face. "Weren't we going to put in an enclosed porch this year? These damn bugs are eating me alive."

"We were. But, you went away." She fell silent.

"I'm sorry," he finally said. "But, I've been making good money. So, call that contractor we've used before, ok? We'll get him to do it."

"Sure. But, that's not the only thing that's bothering you."

"No." He looked around to be sure no neighbours were within earshot. "You know when I got hurt a while back, during the first military job?" He held up his hand that had missing fingers.

She nodded, "Of course. How could I forget?"

"Well, they made me sign confidentiality papers. The consequences could be very dire if I were to break that agreement."

"I know that," she put her hand on his shoulder. "I think it's better that you not speak of those things right now, even though I know they must be weighing on you."

He smiled and said nothing; he couldn't, for fear of his safety, and that of his family.

What would happen if I talked? Likely, I'd end up in a military prison for the rest of my life, or worse. Who knows?

If he were gone, where would his family be then? And, if not that, then he'd surely be black-balled in his field when word got around that he'd violated his security oath. No, Leon decided, he'd have to keep tight-lipped about all that had happened to him since he'd gone to work for the secret military. He just hoped his wife would *really* be able to handle his silence.

He gripped her hand tighter, "You're right. I-I can't talk about it now...maybe one day. It's just too dangerous..."

I'll buy her something nice, and take her and Jennie on a trip. It's the least I can do.

"How'd you like it if we went someplace warm? With a nice beach? The weather is really cooling off here, but Mexico would be nice this time of year. We could use some family time together, what do you think?" he smiled and looked into her eyes.

"That sounds great, hun. I have some time off work coming to me, and we could take Jennie out of school for a few days. Things are slowing down for the end of the year, anyway. It sounds lovely." She came over and sat on his lap, snuggling into him.

"Great, but first, I'm taking you on a shopping spree. Anything you want, new outfits, and some jewelry. We'll do that before the trip!" He smiled big, feeling like a little kid about to go on an adventure. Some time in the sun having fun would be most welcomed.

Might as well live it up some on what I've been earning.

The next day, they had a nice, big home cooked dinner by his wife, and planned their vacation. Then after, the three of them sat around watching movies, something they used to do when he was home more. It was starting to feel like he had a family again. He sat on the couch eating popcorn with his wife, while their daughter lay on the floor, lit up by the glow of the TV.

That night he lay in bed, not able to sleep, staring at the ceiling. His wife woke up to go to the bathroom and noticed he was wake.

"Are you ok?" she asked.

"Awful things are going on in the world, just awful. And most of those things regular people never even see. Never even dream exist. I-I need to get some air," he stood up. He pulled on his clothes and grabbed his car keys.

"Where are you going?"

He shrugged, "I dunno. Just for a drive. I need to clear my head. Maybe see if I can meet up with one of the other guys who was on the job. He lives not too far from here."

"Be careful." She hugged him, but he was distant.

She watched him from the window as his SUV pulled out into the night.

"Mommy, where did daddy go?" Jennie called out from her bed.

"He just went out to the store. He'll be back soon. Go back to sleep." She hoped that Jennie would fall back asleep, and she wouldn't be caught in her lie.

Leon dialed Frank as he drove, glad that he had a hands-free phone in the car. The phone rang and Frank picked up.

"Hello?"

"Frank? It's Leon."

"Leon, how are you buddy?"

They'd not spoken since they got back, and right now he knew Frank was the only person he could talk to who would understand. He sighed with relief. "Sorry, it's late, but I need to talk to you. Can we get together now? It's important." He gripped the wheel tighter with his good hand.

"Sure, want to come over?"

"How about that bar near you? I could use a drink." Frank had told him about a funky little bar that he liked to frequent, and they'd planned to visit it, but hadn't yet.

"Alright. Say a half hour?"

"Sounds good, I'll see you there. And, thanks!" He clicked off the phone. He had just enough time to get to the bar if he hurried. He put his foot down and was glad to be on the road and have the white lines moving by.

The bar was one-of-a-kind, covered with metal scraps and coloured lights. It looked like Christmas in a junkyard. But, the rough exterior kept most "tourists" away, and was generally frequented by a cooler crowd. This suited Leon just fine, and he picked a quiet booth in the back, far away from the action, and ordered a beer.

He had time to take a few sips and was actually starting to relax, watching the multiple TVs that played obscure horror movies with the sound off, as hard rock music thumped from the bar's sound system. A small stage near the front door was being readied for a performance that night from a punk band.

Frank wandered in and waved to him. "Hiya," he said, swinging into the booth.

"Good to see you, Frank."

They shook hands.

"So, we finally made it here, huh? I wasn't sure we'd see the day," Frank said.

"Me either."

The waitress came up and said hello to Frank. She knew what he drank and brought him a beer, and then got one for Leon.

Frank and Leon clinked bottles and drank to their health. After some small talk about their families and what they'd been doing since getting back, Leon leaned over to Frank, "Has anyone contacted you? The General? Maxwell?"

Frank shook his head. "Not a peep, and I like it that way, let me tell you."

"So, I take it you wouldn't go back?"

"Hell, no! I ain't going back down there for any money. It just ain't worth it with...those things there! What good is all the money in the world if you're dead?" He chugged his beer, emptying it and signaled to the waitress who brought over another one.

"Must be nice to be within stumbling distance of your favourite bar!" Leon smiled.

"Yep, but it's hell on the wallet – and liver!" Frank picked up the new bottle and clinked the bottle Leon was still nursing along.

"They've not contacted me yet, but I expect it's coming soon. Why wouldn't they? We've already been down there, and we know what's going on. It's a lot easier to use us again than someone new," Leon said.

"Yeah, but except that I'm not going."

"I don't want to either, but I might have to. I've got a family to think about, you don't." A silence fell between them in the noisy bar. Leon let the music fill the empty space and watched the punk band setting up.

A woman came in and waved to Frank. He forced a smile and waved back.

"I can't forget about what we saw there. I've got a child myself! I think you know what I'm referring to," Leon said.

Frank pulled hard on his second beer, almost killing it. "Of course I do! All those kids, man!"

"We've got to get the word out about it. Something's got to be done to stop it."

Frank leaned over to Leon's ear, "What do you mean "we"? I don't know about you, but I'm not saying a word to anyone. We shouldn't even be talking about this. If someone finds out..." Frank shook his head and waved for another beer.

"I've kept my mouth shut, believe me. But, I don't think I can do it forever."

"Oh, so what are you gonna do?" Frank sat back in the booth and laughed. "Who's gonna believe you, for one? And, two, this is the secret military, shadow government-run system we're talking about here. You start talking and you'll be dog food pretty damn quick. Your family, too!"

The waitress put a full beer on the table and grabbed the empty one. They both tried to smile at her. She was cute. "Another one for you?" she asked Leon.

"No, thanks, I gotta drive. How about a club soda?"

"Sure," she nodded and turned back to the bar.

Frank and Leon dropped their smiles.

"I'm just gonna walk away from this. It's too big and too deep. There's nothing I can do about it. I'll put a letter in my will, and spill all my beans there, but that's as much of a risk I want to take with it," Frank said and drank more beer. "I suggest you do the same."

Leon looked at him. "I guess you're right. I wouldn't be very much use to anyone locked up, or worse."

"Nope."

The waitress brought the club soda. "You're driving. It's on the house."

"Why, thanks!" Leon smiled at her.

"Sure thing," she smiled back and checked Frank's bottle before moving off.

They sat in the booth until the band started. They watched as the band played a couple of buzz-saw like songs and then Leon shouted his goodbye into Frank's ear. He left Frank to drink the night away, wishing he could do the same, but instead he went home and tried to sleep.

He spent most of the night awake, flicking through the TV channels. In the morning he would go back to his office and try to pretend that life was just the same as before.

A few days at the office were enough to make sure everything was alright, and then Leon went away with his family to Mexico for a week. It was a lot of fun, and helped them to get closer again.

By the end of the week of seeing pyramids and getting sun burned on white sand beaches, it was like they had never been apart. But, Leon still had the nightmares to remind him, of Greys chasing him, men being killed in front of him, and dead people frozen in tanks. He often awoke sweating, scared, and out of breath – if he slept at all.

18

Months passed and life continued at a regular pace for Leon. Work had increased for him, and he was making more money than ever with his business. But, he was also more stressed out too, and was having arguments with his wife and staff. Everyone could tell there was something getting to him, but he said nothing to anyone who asked. He slept very little, suffering from severe insomnia, and the terrifying nightmares.

Sleeping pills helped a little, and as time went by he was able to start putting some of the traumatic experiences behind him and get back to his regular life. He kept the cell phone the General had given him turned off.

Halloween came and they dressed Jennie up as a little princess and Mary took her trick or treating around the neighbourhood. Leon stayed home to hand out candy and hoped that none of the children would be dressed up as a Grey – he didn't know if he could take that right then. Thankfully, none did, and he didn't have to drink the whole bottle of Scotch he'd been pouring from to get through it. He actually had a good time in the end, playing The Monster Mash on the stereo, and dancing around with Jennie after she came home with her bag of loot.

Thanksgiving that year was one of the best Leon and his family had ever had, as the extra money he'd made afforded them a lavish spread. Leon felt he had a lot to be thankful for that year, and prayed with his family before cutting the turkey.

Christmas time came and he made sure his family had the best Christmas ever, getting them lots of presents, and having friends and relatives over to visit. With all the festivities, he had almost forgotten about working for the secret military in their underground bases, but they had not forgotten about him.

He often felt that he was being watched, but there was nothing he could prove, just odd cars driving slowly by his house late at night, and clicks on the phone. He expected they were keeping tabs on him, and he knew that they were likely to pay him another visit sometime soon. What he would do, and say to them when they did, he was not sure, but he was in no hurry for it to happen.

He watched the ball drop on TV at midnight, from Times Square on New Year's Eve, with his wife, and surrounded by friends, as the flames crackled away in the fireplace, warding off the ice and snow outside. Kissing Mary at midnight made him realize how lucky he was. Coming close to death had made him appreciate everything in his life that much more.

***

The first week into the new year, he got another visit from Mr. Black. Leon had arrived into his office, banging snow off his shoes, when Nancy waved him over.

"There's someone in your office. That same man from before – you remember? The creepy one? Dressed all in black, with that old suit?" she scrunched up her face.

The Man in Black. Mr. Black.

"Oh? I think so," he said, and took off his coat. He went to the kitchen first and got himself a big cup of coffee. He knew who it was. Taking a few deep breaths, he tried to calm himself down before entering his office.

He walked from the kitchen slowly, so as not to spill his coffee, and to take as much time as possible before the confrontation. He rounded the corner to his office and saw the door open, and the edge of a black Fedora beyond the open door. Mr. Black had added a hat to his wardrobe. Leon gulped and felt his stomach tighten. His palms were sweaty and he was also breaking into a sweat all over. Taking a deep breath, he stepped into his office.

"Hello, Leon! Nice to see you again," Mr. Black said, taking his feet off Leon's desk and offering his hand.

He shook it gingerly and closed the door. He stepped behind his desk. "This is a surprise. But, then I shouldn't be surprised anymore, I guess." Leon sat down.

"You're learning, Leon," the man said, not smiling.

"What brings you here? Haven't I been through enough?" He rubbed his hand with the missing fingers.

The man nodded. "You have been through a lot. And, you've done and seen a lot. That's why we value you..."

Leon cut him off, "I know why you're here. What if I told you that I didn't want to go back to work for you?"

The man stared at him for a long moment. "That would mean that we'd have to spend a lot of time and money finding someone to replace you. I wouldn't advise it, personally."

"Well, you're not me. I'm flattered that I'm thought of so highly, but really, I think I'm done."

"That may be what *you* think, but it's not the case," the man smirked slightly.

Though, if I go back, I might be able to do something about those dead people; those dead, frozen children. Maybe stop the Greys from taking any more. It might be worthwhile.

Leon didn't like that the guy was enjoying making him squirm. "And, why is that?"

"I guess you didn't read your contract very closely. It says that your employment with us is "at will". That is, at *our* will. And, we *will* have you back with us. How soon can you start?"

"Look, I'm happy with my life as it is. Things are just getting back to normal and..."

"Normal is a relative term, as I'm sure you know by now."

"Yes, but..."

"All those frozen people, taken by the Greys, for experiments, or maybe for food...Are you telling me you can honestly walk away when you know that we've got a problem of that magnitude on our hands, Leon?" He had him there.

Leon sipped his coffee, and his head pounded. He feared that more people would meet the same fate. "I don't doubt it's going to be an ongoing problem, but I don't know if I'm the man for the job. I just don't know..." He shook his head as the terrible images filled his mind, and his nerves went raw with reawakened pains in his body. His heart was racing, and adrenaline flowed into his veins with the thoughts of what he'd been through in those tunnels.

The Man in Black waited patiently, quietly. He knew how to appeal to Leon's conscience and what buttons to push. "I know you don't want to go back down there. No one really would in your position. I get that. But, if you just throw away your experiences with...them, then it will be a great loss to our cause. With your help we can stop them just that much sooner. And, the world will be a safer place for your family and for families everywhere. Don't worry, we'll pay you more, too!"

Like he's reading my mind!

Leon nodded. "I hear you," he sighed. "What's the deal this time?"

Mr. Black smiled and laid out the plan to Leon: he'd be needed to brief and help lead a reconnaissance mission back into the tunnels, to recover the bodies of the frozen humans, and to chart the progress of the Grey's retreat. They had pulled back into their own deeper tunnels, away from the military's tunnels, but just how far they had gone was not known. The Grey's had developed advanced jamming and cloaking technology, and no radar the military had could find their current location; the only way was to search down below the surface in person.

After he finished explaining it all to Leon, he handed him an envelope with a wad of cash in it. He knew all along that Leon would accept the new assignment, that he didn't have much of a choice.

Still, Leon could have flatly refused and gone to prison – people had done it before. But, they were usually single men, without a family, and with not as much to lose. Mr. Black was confident in his powers of persuasion and was pleased that he'd been proven right, again.

"Be seeing you," the Man in Black said on his way out of the office, tipping his hat. Leon sat at his desk while the man left, not bothering to walk him out. He listened to the squeak of the man's perfectly polished shoes on the tile floor, him saying goodbye to the receptionist, and the outer door as it swung shut behind him.

Leon stood at the window and watched the big, old, but in perfect condition, black Lincoln with tinted windows drive away. The sun looked too bright through the Venetian blinds, reflecting off the snow, and it glinted off the chrome of the car. He thought he saw the Man in Black smiling at him as he drove away, but he couldn't be sure.

Leon had a headache, so he took something for it, washing it down with coffee. There was no way he was going to be able to concentrate on work that day, so he called up Frank to see if they could meet.

It was good timing, as Frank told him that he had also been visited by Mr. Black and was considerably freaked out. They agreed to meet at Frank's local bar, again.

"I just don't know," Frank fretted. "What's gonna happen if we go down there again? Who's knows if we'll come back? Jeez, how did we get ourselves into this?" Frank slugged hard on his beer, spilling some on his chin. He wiped it off with a hard motion, frustrated at himself.

"I guess we were happy to serve our country. But, then it turned into something even they didn't know about," Leon shrugged.

"You so sure about that?" Frank snorted.

"What? That they knew about...them?"

"Yeah, that's precisely what I'm talking about!"

Leon thought he looked ready to explode into a rage at any moment. "Look, just try and relax, ok? Whether they did, or not, it doesn't make any difference now. What we've seen, how can we just ignore it? I can't." He took a sip of his beer and looked around the bar, at the flashing Christmas lights over the cash register, the Mother Mary statue painted blue in an alcove above that, and at the TVs playing 70's movies with the sound off. There was music coming from the large speakers, hard and pounding. It gave him energy and tightened his resolve that he had to do something to help.

"No, I can't ignore it either," Frank said, "as much as I'd like to. Dammit!"

"So, you're going back, too?"

"I guess so, I mean, what can I do? I don't want to go to prison."

"Military prison."

"We are kinda screwed," Frank said.

"But even if we weren't, I think we're going back for a good cause. Those poor people, and the children...I can't let that go on."

"Nope, me neither," Frank threw up his hands. "And, if those...things," he looked around, to make sure no one was listening, "...are really taking our side by surprise, that's a very frightening thought."

"Do you think there's a way we can actually stop them? Stop those things from happening again?"

"I dunno," Frank said, "that depends if you buy what they told us."

"If we can trust them, you mean?"

"Yeah. I'm not sure they even know what's going on, and if they don't, they hide it pretty well."

"You don't think they told us the whole truth about what's been going on down there?"

"Probably not. They usually function on a need to know basis, and until you need to know, you won't. But, I really don't know. Maybe they did. Maybe they were as surprised as us by what we found. I can't see them letting a thing like that go on if they knew about it. That would be a big security risk right under their noses. If we're gonna go back, we're gonna have to decide to trust them, aren't we?"

"I guess so."

Frank raised his beer and they clinked their bottles together. "Here's to us getting back safe and doing some good," he said.

"Amen to that," Leon answered and drank the rest of his beer.

The waitress brought them a couple more and they didn't talk about the upcoming mission much, just about what they were going to do when it was all over and they were back home again. They ordered some food, and considered the very real fact that it might be one of their last meals aboveground.

Leon bid goodbye to Frank and got into his car to drive home. Their orders would have them together again in less than two weeks time, back at the same base.

Leon took the long way home. He needed time to think, alone. The stars were bright and as much as he loved the dirt and being underground, he loved the night sky, too. He had always liked to look at the stars and wonder about the origin of humanity and if there were others out there; now he knew the answer. He just wished it was an answer he liked.

He pulled into a roadside diner, a remnant from the fifties of his childhood, with its chrome décor, and thick milkshakes; the kind of place his dad used to take him to. Now, his father was old and had too many health problems to drive. It had been tough on his dad to give up his car and it was one of the only times he had ever seen his father cry.

Leon had a burger, onion rings, and a big, chocolate milkshake. He was overweight, but he enjoyed every bit of it.

It might be one of your last meals...

He ate slowly, sitting under the glaring fluorescent lights, as teenagers in booths nearby joked around.

I was young and careless once, too.

But now, if he wanted the chance for his daughter and other kids like her to grow up to be teenagers and do the same, he knew he had to go back underground and stop the Greys, no matter what happened to him. No one said being a hero was going to be easy, but the job had come to Leon and he was going to do his best to see it through.

Long live freedom!

He smiled and waved to the waitress on his way out, feeling good that he was being given the chance to make a positive difference in the world.

He drove home and went into the house as quietly as he could, so as not to wake Jennie. He knew his wife would be a light sleeper when he was gone, and would likely be awake when he got home. He looked in at Jennie as she slept and smiled to himself. Then, he went into his bedroom and started to change for bed.

His wife stirred, "Hi. You ok?"

"Yep. I met up with Frank."

"Oh, how's he doing?"

"Alright. We had a good talk."

He turned on the light on the side table and sat on the bed. He took his wife's hands in his. "I've got something to tell you, and I know you're not going to like it, but please, hear me out and try to understand."

Then, he told her he had to go away again, and would be leaving soon.

19

Back at the base, Leon and Frank were reunited with Maxwell and the General. They were given new uniforms and issued updated laser rifles; the Remi EPR2.

"These are better. They cut up the Greys in half the time," Maxwell boasted, only half-joking, handing out the new guns on the firing range.

When they fired the new guns, they were impressed. Leon did think they were an improvement, and thought that he would enjoy using them on any Greys they might encounter.

"A good Grey is a dead Grey, huh?" Frank pulled the trigger, blowing the target to bits, of a cutout Grey.

After the firing range, Maxwell led them into the briefing room. The General sat at the back of the room with Leon and Frank, who were the only ones, apart from Maxwell, that had any combat experience with the Greys.

Maxwell addressed the green troops – only green in the sense that they had not encountered Greys; they were all military and Special Forces trained. "Gentleman, most of you are wondering why you are here, in this secure facility, way out in the desert. For many of you this is a first visit to this kind of base. I expect you to be a bit amazed by this, as it *is* an impressive feat, what we have engineered here. But, this is only the start, as you are going to see." He paused and looked to the General, who gave a wave of his hand, as to continue. "The General feels it's time that I brief you on the mission, so brace yourselves."

Maxwell then turned on a projector and displayed pictures of the massive tunnel network under the base, stretching out for miles in multiple directions. Most of the troops had only heard rumours of D.U.M.B.s, like some civilians had. Security was tight on projects such as these, and little evidence ever got out to the surface, mostly just hearsay. So, the troops were glued to Maxwell's information, and some even had their mouths fall open as the implications of what they were being told hit them. Many questions entered their minds: How far did the tunnels go? What were they connected to? How much did it all cost and who built it? But, those answers were not being given at this time.

Once Maxwell had finished his introduction to the tunnels, the General stepped up to the front of the room. This made the troops even more attentive. Maxwell passed the projector controller to him. If the revelations about the tunnels had gotten their attention, what the General was going to tell them next would blow their minds.

"Thank you, Sergeant Maxwell," the General said. An image of one of the tunnels was on the screen, and he stepped across the projection of the beam. "What I am going to tell you now, you may have a hard time believing. But, I can assure you it is true. I have seen them myself, and others in the room here have as well, they have even battled them. I won't mince words; we have discovered the presence of extraterrestrial aliens underground." He flipped to a picture of a dead Grey.

"Hey, it's an E.T.!" one of the soldiers quipped from the darkness.

"I wish they were as warm and fuzzy. But, how they knew about them for that movie before we did, I don't know," the General paused for effect. "They are called Greys. They are evil, bent on human destruction and it is your mission to destroy any that you encounter. Leon, please come up here," the General shielded his eyes from the beam coming from the projector and looked for Leon at the back of the room.

Leon walked to the front and stood next to the General.

"Can we have the lights, please?" the General asked.

Frank flipped the room lights back on.

"Leon, can you tell them what happened to you down in the tunnels, and show them your wounds, please?"

Leon looked over the group of about twenty soldiers, all staring at him. It was obvious to them that something was strange with his hand. He held up his hand with the missing fingers, "I was on a mission down in the tunnels a few months ago, and we met some Greys. They did this to me with their ray guns. And, this." He lifted his shirt and showed them the deep scars on his chest. Even these tough men were taken aback.

He continued, "The Greys are foul beings who wish to kill humans. I'm lucky I escaped with my life. I'm going back into the tunnels to help with the clean up of their base that we found. I don't think we'll see anymore of them there, but who knows? We were surprised last time. We killed the Greys we encountered down there and there were no more left in the base. Some escaped, to where, we are not sure, yet."

The General changed the screen to show pictures of the aftermath of the battle Leon had been in; the wounded, dead, and bloodied humans on the ground, and the charred Grey bodies. Then, the Grey's base, looking very much like a hive on the outside, and a horror-movie nightmare on the inside. The troops stared with open fascination, and also with more than a little fear.

"I'm going back, because we found something even more horrible there, and we've got to do what we can to stop it," he looked at the General.

The General changed the picture to show the frozen humans in the tanks. A murmur went through the soldiers.

"I'm afraid it's all too real. For unknown reasons, we found a great number of humans, frozen in tanks of liquid inside the

Grey's lair. We're going back to recover them, so we can learn what we can about why the Greys did this, and find out how to stop them. I'm sure their families would like some closure, too. I have a daughter of my own, and I know it's my duty to make the world a better place for her, and for her children. Those of you who have families of your own, I know you will better understand this. But, I want to thank you all for your service." Leon went back to his seat.

"Thank you, Leon," the General said, and shut off the projector. "Get some rest tonight, all of you. Tomorrow the mission will begin."

The troops started to get up and chairs rattled across the floor.

"One more thing," the General called out.

Everyone stopped.

"Due to the dangers involved in this operation, I'm going to have to ask for all non-military people here to get a microchip tracker placed in your bodies; those who are military should already have something suitable. It's for your own safety, if you should get lost down in the tunnels."

"I'm not getting any microchip put into me." Frank said. "That wasn't in my contract! No, way!"

"Relax," the General held his hand up. "We don't have to do it that way. There are a couple of options, including a very small tracker we can attach to one of your teeth. We can glue it on, and it's so small that you won't even know it's there. When you are done with the mission, we'll take it right out. Or, for those of you who don't have a problem with a subdermal implant, we can put the tracker right under the skin in your hand. It's up to you, but I insist that everyone get a tracker at this point. Those who need a tracker, follow me."

The General lead Leon, Frank, and a few other civilians into the medical wing. They all opted to have the temporary tooth tracker installed, as there had been a lot of talk going around that they were living in the End Times, and they'd have to take the "mark of the beast" in their head, or hand.

After the tracker procedure, Leon went back to his room to rest. The presentation had been taxing on him.

Soon, Frank knocked on the door of Leon's suite.

Leon stirred, coming out of his nap, "Come on in."

Frank opened the door, looked around and took a seat. "I see the accommodations haven't changed since our last visit," he grinned.

"No, they have had other things to waste our tax money on, I guess," Leon smiled, sitting up on the bed. He'd been laying on the top of the covers, watching TV, when he'd dozed off.

"How's the outside world doing?" Frank looked at the TV.

"Looks like it's still there."

"Ah, that's good. I'd like someplace to go back to when this is all over."

A silence fell between them. They were both thinking of tomorrow morning's mission.

"I don't think I'll sleep much tonight, what about you?" Frank asked.

"I doubt it."

Frank sat back and let his thoughts unfurl, "This whole thing has been eye-opening for me. When I started, I was an engineer, and figured that I had everything pretty much figured out. But now? I'm not sure what to think about most things. Maybe those conspiracy theories are all real! Damn, once you find out that aliens are real and they are here, then anything seems plausible. Maybe time travel is real, and teleportation, too? Maybe cloning is well advanced? Maybe there is a hollow Earth, too? Who knows? With those aliens around, the Earth could be taken out at any time, so I'm going to enjoy the time I have left and not worry about it all too much. If it's my time to go, I'll go!"

"That's a good way to put it. I feel pretty much the same. Like Warren Zevon said: "Enjoy every sandwich." I think that's good advice, especially when you're fool enough to go back into tunnels with aliens who almost killed you before."

Frank laughed. "We must be nuts, huh?"

He found himself chuckling along, "Yeah, buddy. I guess we must be!"

***

The next morning after breakfast, Maxwell led the team to the elevator that took them down to the deep tunnels. This time, everyone had small video cameras mounted on their helmets, as everything was being recorded.

Leon and Frank stuck close together – at least they knew they could trust each other, if anything happened. As for the others, though they looked quite capable, they couldn't be sure of them.

The maglev came, with a much bigger train car this time, so the whole group could fit into one car. It was outfitted with special cutting gear, piles of stretchers, and black body bags. Maxwell led them aboard and the doors hissed closed.

Leon watched as the tunnel sped by the windows, breaking out in a slight sweat. Frank looked a bit nervous too, as did Maxwell. The three were the only ones who had contact with the Greys, so they knew what they were getting into. The new soldiers didn't fully know what they had to be afraid of.

Maxwell watched the control panels, and made sure the maglev stopped at the right point. The scope was clear for any living things.

"Ok, folks. It's looking fine out there, but look alive. Have your rifles ready to fire at any time. Remember, if you see any Greys, shoot first and shoot to kill. Grab some body bags and stretchers. We'll take the first load out." He picked up his rifle, opened the door and led the group out into the tunnel.

The slight, warm wind in the tunnel hit Leon in the face, and he thought he smelled the Grey's stink on the air, but he was probably imaging it. They hopped into the Humvees and went down the tunnel to the end.

There were no Grey bodies at the end of the tunnel, near the boring machine, as a cleanup crew had come by and picked them up, so they could be studied.

Leon coughed as dust tickled his throat. Frank thumped him lightly on the back in a joking gesture and he nodded that he was ok. Up ahead, they could see the part of the tunnel that Maxwell had sealed over the last time they were here.

Now, Maxwell blasted at the seal, opening the tunnel wall up again. The first thing they noticed once the seal was broken was the stink. The rotting Grey bodies had been decomposing in the cavern for some time. Most of the group started to cough and retch.

Maxwell stepped into the hole he had just uncovered. "Come on you pussies, it ain't that bad! You and you, stay here and guard the Humvees." He pointed to two of the recruits who looked the most taken aback by the smell.

"It *is* that bad!" Frank complained to Leon, covering his nose with his sleeve. "Why don't they give us some kind of masks?"

They followed Maxwell into the Grey's cavern, and thankfully, the stink died down; there was a positive air pressure and it forced most of the stink out past them, through the hole, and away. The Grey's tunnel was still lit by the glow from the light-emitting moss that seemed to grow everywhere.

Maxwell pointed to the moss. "Get a sample of that," he told one of the soldiers.

The soldier took a plastic bag out of his pocket and broke off some of the moss into the bag, then sealed it up, to bring back to the surface.

The group moved slowly across the open area toward the Grey's building, hauling stretchers with body bags on them, stepping over decomposing bodies and bones of Greys that had been whole bodies only a short time ago; it seemed they rotted fast.

"Shouldn't we take some of these bones?" the soldier with the sampling kit asked.

"No, we have enough Grey bodies already. Let's keep moving," Maxwell said. He crept forward, looking over the Grey's dark, hive-like building as it came into clear view. There was no sign of anything moving, and his portable scanner did not show anything alive. The troops who had not been there before stared at the Grey's building.

Maxwell posted most of the team outside to guard the entrance, and took Leon, Frank, and couple of the others inside, carrying stretchers between them.

It was still eerie, as they walked through the hallways of the alien base, and Leon didn't like it one bit. He again got the impression that it was like walking in the belly of a perverted whale; struts ran up the walls and over the ceiling, like black bones, on black, shiny skin. He shuddered. Even worse, he knew where they were headed, and what they would find there. The lights in the hallways were off this time, probably having ran their batteries down, and they turned on the lights on their helmets, and at the end of their guns.

They came to the room with the frozen human bodies in it. Maxwell told the others to stay outside the room, then he nodded at Leon and Frank, and pointed his gun towards the door. Leon opened it and carefully walked in with his rifle out in front.

He immediately saw the tanks in the beam of his rifle light.

But, now, the bodies were floating, as the frozen liquid had melted. They bobbed around in slow motion, decomposing. It stank horribly in there.

"Oh, Christ!" Leon gasped. His stomach turned in knots and he felt sick. He took a quick glance at the tanks, but he didn't want to look at them for long.

"God, it's horrible," Frank faltered, and then dry heaved.

"Get it together ladies," said Maxwell, pulling several small, cutting torches from the pouch on his belt.

"What are those?" Leon asked.

"What do you think? We're gonna cut that tank open!" Maxwell almost yelled at him.

"No, way!" Frank said.

"What do you think we came back here for?" Maxwell asked. He put down some body bags and got a cutting torch ready.

Frank just shrugged.

Maxwell handed a torch each to Leon and Frank. "I'm thinking we start on the ends. What do you think?"

Leon looked at the tank and nodded, "That would be my guess." He examined the torch and tried to fire it up.

That's when Maxwell's scanner started going crazy and beeping.

"What the hell?" Maxwell shouted. He adjusted some of the controls, but it kept beeping and he could see many dots, indicating life forms, probably Greys, moving to surround the base. He clicked on his microphone: "Perimeter team, do you copy the scanner warnings?" He listened for a response.

"Roger that, inner team! We have multiple incoming bogeys. Unknown what they are, but they are coming in fast, all around us! Oh, shit, I can see them now, they're Greys!" The transmission cut off with the sound of laser rifles firing and men screaming.

"Shit!" Maxwell said.

The soldiers who had been outside the door were now down the hall, on their stomachs, trading laser fire with the Greys. Maxwell moved to the door and watched as the overwhelming number of Greys cut them all to pieces. He tried to return fire, but the laser blasts that hit the wall right near him were coming too fast.

Maxwell slammed the door shut. He grabbed Leon and Frank, pulling them behind the tanks. "Our men are all dead out there! We need to get some cover!"

"Why don't we get out of here, if they're coming?" Frank's voice was getting high, panicked, and he was sweating.

"Because, they're in the goddamn hallway and there's too many of them! Any of them comes in that door, they're dead meat!" Maxwell checked his rifle and steadied it on the side of a tank, pointing at the door. The others took aim, also.

"Request reinforcements!" Maxwell shouted into his microphone, over and over again. But, only static came back over the headphones.

Maxwell checked the scanner and it kept beeping.

"How many of them are coming?" Leon asked.

"Lots! Maybe forty," Maxwell dripped sweat off his nose and onto the screen.

"Holy, shit!" Frank stared at the door and gripped his rifle.

"We killed more than that last time, didn't we boys?" Maxwell grinned, and looked at Leon and Frank, trying to boost their spirits.

"We did," Leon said.

"I guess we did, yeah," Frank had to admit.

They hid there, behind the tanks, waiting for the aliens to enter the room and attack.

They didn't have long to wait, as a few moments later the door opened slightly and a projectile flew into the room. It was a small rocket and it clanged to a stop against the tank they were hiding behind. They all ducked for cover, but it didn't explode, just started to hiss and give off a white gas that soon filled the room, and rendered them all unconscious.

After they were knocked out, several Greys entered the room. They walked over to the comatose humans, on their thin, stick-like legs, and peered down at them on the ground with their large, unblinking, almond-shaped, deep black eyes. Their grey faces showed no emotion, their tiny mouths unmoving, lending even more to the theory that they were biological robots, programmed, or controlled to accomplish a task. Using a small, anti-gravity device, they floated the humans inches from the floor and out into the hallway, and then took them deeper into their hive complex.

They stopped in front of a door, and one of them passed its spindly, alien hand over a sensor. The door opened to reveal an elevator. They pulled the humans inside, then the door closed, and the elevator descended even deeper underground, to link up with another part of the Grey's tunnel system.

20

A while later, Leon awoke in the dark. He could hear the hissing of air conditioning and it stunk slightly of Greys, but weaker, and the air was cool. He shivered. He was naked and alone, and it felt like he was laying on a cold, steel floor. He coughed a lot. He felt dizzy.

Where am I?

Soon, he felt strong enough to sit up. He could hear muffled sounds, but nothing very clear. His head hurt, like he had a bad hangover, and he was thirsty.

Suddenly, he remembered what had happened, and he had to stop himself from screaming, once he realized where he must be.

His heart was pounding with fear.

He rubbed his eyes and could make out a dim window in a door ahead of him. He was in a small cell, with nothing else in it. All of his equipment was gone, so he could not defend himself, or call for help.

He felt weak and lay back down on the floor. He guessed he must be inside the Grey base, maybe the one they had been captured in, or maybe moved to another one, he had no way to tell. For all he knew, he was on one of their UFOs.

His tongue traced the location of the microchip on his tooth. He breathed a sigh of relief that it was still there. At least they could, maybe, track him, and find him. But, whether the room he was in was shielded to prevent it from transmitting a signal, he didn't know.

Oh, God! Help me!

All he could do was pray that it would still work.

He put his hands together and kept praying. He closed his eyes, even though it was almost pitch black in there. He thought of Mary and Jennie, and prayed that he hadn't done a foolish thing, the wrong thing, by coming back down into the tunnels again. He thought of Frank, Maxwell, and the other soldiers who had been with him, and wondered what had become of them. He was afraid as he lay there, alone in the dark, a prisoner of the Greys.

His breath started to come in fast bursts, with panic.

He tried to calm himself down. He told himself that the only chance he had of escape was if he could retain his judgment.

Hang on, Leon, there are people counting on you!

He hoped the aliens couldn't read minds, as he was thinking some pretty nasty things to do to them when they opened the door.

But, the door didn't open, and he got even more tired, hungry, and thirsty as the hours dragged on.

He wondered if they were just going to let him die in there.

They were probably watching him now, he imagined, on cameras, having a good time watching him suffer. He didn't know why they seemed to hate humans so much, and treated them so badly. Maybe there were things that had happened between humans and the Greys that he didn't know about; some old, secret conflict. He realized that there were now a great many things in the world, and in the universe, that he didn't know anything about.

He tried to conserve his energy as much as possible. He did some deep breathing to stay calm, and tried to keep alert for any chance that he got to escape – if he got any at all.

The military would know they were missing soon, and send a rescue team, he hoped. He was pretty sure they would, even if it was a secret mission. There were too many people involved, and too much at stake not to mount a rescue mission, he reasoned. He just hoped he was still alive when they found him.

There was no telling what the Greys were going to do to him; maybe torture him for information, or just for fun, if they had fun. Use him for experiments? He didn't think they were going to kill him, or they'd have done that already, probably. But, he didn't really know. Judging by the people he'd seen in the tanks, they had strange uses for humans – maybe they ate humans, and maybe he'd be one of them. The thought of having to be in close contact with any of them again froze him to his core.

All he could do was lay in the dark, alone, and wait. He tried not to think about how he was probably miles underground and a prisoner.

"Please, God. If there's a way out of here, let me find it," he whispered quietly.

He imagined the Greys watching him, listening, and laughing at his prayers.

This is the worst thing in my life!

If he got out of this alive, then the rest of his life would be gravy.

He thought about what he'd do when the door opened, and turned the possibilities over, and over in his mind. None of them seemed really good, as even if he did manage to get out of this room, there were bound to be many Greys around, blocking his escape. And, he had no idea where he was, miles underground, in some strange tunnel system...

He just hoped the cavalry was coming, and soon.

Continued in book 2 Oceandeep.

Author's Note

Millions of people claim they have seen a Grey alien and/or a UFO – they can't all be lying, or crazy, can they?

This story comes out of a long fascination I've had with stories of aliens and UFOs. There are so many sci-fi stories (and also accounts that people claim that are real) to do with these topics, that they are very hard to ignore. Many of these stories deal with extraterrestrial beings called the Greys.

Some of the stories of aliens (usually Greys) have been heartwarming, but even they carried elements that were terrifying and food for nightmares. There is just something about the stories of aliens that fires the imagination. Maybe it's because many of us think there must be other races out there – and maybe they are not like us at all. Maybe not all of them are friendly, either.

There are a lot of clues that point to contacts between humanity and aliens in our past. A lot of them make a lot of sense, I think. However, hard proof remains elusive for many people, while others are convinced. In any case, the topic is very intriguing to many, myself included.

Tales about aliens frequently contain the "creepy" factor, just for the fact that they are foreign to us, and the unknown can often be scarey. Plus, sometimes they *look* frightening and do frightening things! I remember reading books and seeing movies when I was younger that had aliens resembling Greys, many of which were creepy, with horror-movie type of scenes in them, designed to frighten. A lot of these books were best-sellers and the movies blockbusters, so there was a big demand for them. I've had a vivid imagination since I was a young child, and used to have nightmares. So, seeing these movies and books probably just helped to add fuel to my nightmares!

I even scared myself writing this story! But, many of us like to be scared now and then. Maybe it makes our daily lives more "normal" and comforting. Though, daily life these days is getting more like a sci-fi story all the time!

I have ideas for 2 more parts to this story (maybe more), so if you liked this one, and want more, let me know! I'll be more apt to get them out in a timely manner if I know people are waiting to read them! Plus, it's always good to hear from readers who enjoyed my work.

Dave

April 2013

www.DavidSloma.com

P.S. I've got an email newsletter subscription box on my site, where you can sign up for news of upcoming releases, and receive special offers for subscribers only.

P.P.S. While every effort is made to find and correct typos in the manuscript prior to publication, this is a very difficult task to get 100% right. I constantly find typos in best-selling and classic books, newspapers, and magazines. Please, if you find any typos in my books, let me know, and I'll give you a free ebook of mine, of your choice. Contact me at www.DavidSloma.com

Also by David Sloma:

Oceandeep: D.U.M.B.s (Deep Underground Military Bases) – Book 2
Rescueplan: D.U.M.B.s (Deep Underground Military Bases) – Book 3 (coming soon)
Brainjob (novel)
Deathsun 2012 (novella)
David Sloma - Short Stories Volume 1
Chewy, Gooey, Fruit Things (screenplay)
DEATHSUN 2012 (screenplay)
BOI MEETS GRL - a vampire screenplay
ONE JOURNEY (short screenplay)
The Cask Of Amontillado (a modern screenplay of the Poe classic)
KHAOTICA (screenplay)
A Conspicuous Medium - (poems)
Nonfic 1 (nonfiction collection)
Robot Town (novella)
Boi Meets Grl – a vampire story (novel)
And, several short stories on their own.

See www.DavidSloma.com for an updated list and to join the email newsletter.